DEADLY LAZER
EXPLODATHON

VINCE KRAMER

D0732438

Thicke & Vaney Press

Purveyors of Fair to Middling Works

What follows is some serious and legally binding shit:
THICKE & VANEY BOOKS
P. O. Box 16305
Saint Paul, MN 55116
thickeandvaneybooks.com
The ISBN is 978-0-9981504-5-1
T&V No. is 1518
Copyright Vince Kramer
Art by Hauke Vagt
Edited by G. Arthur Brown

For Gary. Thanks for coming up with
a title that spoofs my other books.
I wrote a book based on it.

And a big thanks to Bix Skahill, Carlton Mellick
III, Kevin Shamel, William Perkins, Jason Rizos,
Ross Blanchard, everyone who's ever bought
a book, everyone who's bought a calendar, my
mother - JoAnn Kramer, and my father, Budd -
the big Viking king. (R.I.P.)

Please stop haunting Western Trails Ranch.
Come haunt me in Portland instead.
That would be awesome.

Love you all,

        -Vince

PROLOGUE CHAPTER

Paramount Studios, Los Angeles, California,
Timedate: May 2nd, 1967

"DEATH TO STAR TREK!" screamed a member of ISIS as he burst onto the set of Star Trek with an explosive vest and pressed the detonator.

An explosion rocked the sound stage where the cast members were rehearsing an attack scene on the bridge of their fake sci-fi starship, the U.S.S. Enterprise. They usually acted out an attack on the ship by rocking back and forth and pretending they were off balance, but the explosion shook the set for real and tossed them around like they were loose action figures.

Everyone was excited that the show got renewed for a second season. And new cast member Walter Koenig was especially excited to be joining the cast. He was decapitated as the cables of a lighting rig snapped and swooped down from the ceiling, sending his head flying at William Shatner in his captain's chair behind him. The young and attractive lead actor ducked just in time, and then immediately felt his head to make sure his hair wasn't messed up.

George Takei had flown head first clear over

his console. As the smoke cleared he could see more terrorists spilling onto the set from the stage exit. They each held an oversized lazer rifle that looked like they were from straight out of the prop department. Their long beards and turbans were strangely juxtaposed with mirrored goggles and the silvery-colored smocks they were dressed in.

"Oh my!" George exclaimed. He crawled behind the console to hide.

The terrorists screamed their battle cry in unison, "LA ILAH ELA ALLAH!!!!" which just sounded like *LALALALALALALA* in their thick ISIS accents.

The rest of the cast had barely recovered from the explosion enough to see how badly they were banged up when a barrage of lazer blasts started coming right at them, all like *ZAP ZAP ZAP!!! YOU'RE GOING TO DIE!!!* Everyone ducked for cover as tiny explosions and fires broke out wherever the lazers hit. There were so many lazers flying everywhere it was like some sort of DEADLY LAZER EXPLODATHON.

A crew member (not a U.S.S. Enterprise crew member, but a production assistant) got a lazer through the eye and it came out the back of the skull and grazed William Shatner's shoulder. The crewman turned to him and got out the word, "William..."

But before the production assistant could fall down and die, the irked actor snapped, "That's *MISTER* Shatner!" appalled that such a lowly crew member would have the gall to address him by his first name.

The crew member slumped down to the floor in death and *Mister* Shatner went *hmph*, like he got what he deserved.

The split second of joy was quickly interrupted by the screams of his favorite costar, Leonard Nimoy, as an ISIS terrorist carved off his ears with a large Bowie knife. Blood poured down his neck.

"ALLAHU ACKBAR!" the terrorist screamed, holding up the pointy ears—prosthetics glued to the actor to supposedly make him appear alien. Leonard Nimoy held his ear holes and screamed as the blood poured out, all super whiny-like. The prosthetics were so realistic they gave the illusion that the actor might have actually been an alien the whole time.

William Shatner slipped back into character without even thinking about it.

"SPOCK!" he yelled, reaching out for his best friend.

Leonard Nimoy must've felt like doing the same thing, because he reached out too and screamed, "CAPTAIN! HELP ME!!!"

But William Shatner was just embarrassed by how much Leonard was fucking up his final performance by putting too much emotion in it: the actor was playing an alien that was supposed to be devoid of emotion.

But before Leonard Nimoy could curse himself for messing up so bad, the terrorist started cutting through his neck with what appeared to be a... *gigantic lazer sword?* It was 1967 and *Star Wars* wouldn't be out for another decade, so that seemed like a great name for it.

Anyway, Leonard Nimoy's pitiful and bitchy screams wound down as disgusting gurgling as he choked on the blood filling up his severed windpipe. As his eyes rolled back, his head came free with a wet snap in the terrorist's hand.

The terrorist held up the severed head and undulated his war cry again *("LA ILAH ELA ALLAH"),* and then screamed, "NO JEW SHALL WALK AROUND WITH A HEAD ON THEIR SHOULDERS! THIS IS NO GOOD! *JIHAD!"*

William Shatner almost pissed himself because he was Jewish and also had a head on his shoulders just like his friend. He had never felt so vulnerable and afraid for his head.

He wouldn't have to worry about it much longer as another member of ISIS screamed "ALLAHU AKBAR!" and shot him in the face. The hot lazer blast melted William Shatner's face clean off, and it ran down his shirt like runny eggs. An eyeball fell out of its socket and plopped onto the mess, sticking there in the gelatinous goop. But at least his hair still looked good.

George Takei looked almost delighted as he cowered behind his console, having had a full view of the carnage.

That will teach him to shut up, he thought.

George had often fantasized about doing the

same thing to the show's lead actor, like whenever he called him "George *the gay*." It always hurt his feelings a lot. William Shatner was really nothing but a mean prick. George couldn't help but smile as he hid in his safe spot. A world without a William Shatner would be a good world indeed.

Two ISIS members grabbed Nichelle Nichols, the actress that played communications officer Uhura on the show.

"Why are you doing this, man?" she asked. "It's the Sixties!"

"SATTAR TURIK HI'ASWA EARAD MIN 'AY WAQT MADAA," the terrorist responded in all capital letters.

"LA BD MIN TADMIR!" the other declared in his thick ISIS accent.

Nichelle Nichols gasped. She had done a lot of research for her role as a communications officer, and had learned to speak several languages fluently. One of these happened to be Arabic. So, she heard what they were really saying. And it was along the lines of, "Star Trek is the worst show ever. It must be destroyed!"

Nichelle was flabbergasted. They had just been renewed for a second season! She thought everyone liked it. Before she could continue thinking about that thought, she was dragged away by the two men, presumably to be raped really bad because that's probably what terrorists do to women they don't immediately kill.

George Takei assumed the same thing as he

watched her get taken away, and thought, *Oh my!*

Carnage still filled the room all around them as people died and lazers exploded everything, and equipment came crashing down everywhere, spreading fire and death and chaos as terrorists screamed in Arabic and shot lazers everywhere.

Out of the smoke emerged a mysterious figure. He had a big mess of shock white hair sprouting from his head, strange goggles like elaborate telescoping binoculars, and a white laboratory coat.

He approached the cowering actor who played Lieutenant Sulu, seemingly knowing exactly where he was hiding. He reached his hand out to George Takei.

"Come with me if you..." The man lost his train of thought and had to pause to think about it. Then he suddenly got it, and his eyes lit up.

"OH! Come with me if you want to *die!* Die a horrible death! Die a horrible death in an experiment where you don't get to live! *AHHAHAHAHA!!!*" he laughed maniacally.

"*NOOOO!*" George Takei screamed in terror.

The man shrugged and turned away, and ISIS descended on the terrified actor in seconds, shooting him to death with blue lazers that exploded all over his body and made him die.

As the light left George's eyes, the white-haired man was nowhere to be seen. It was like he had just disappeared completely. As if he wasn't even there...

But he *was* there. He popped out of the smoke

and caught a member of ISIS by surprise. He grabbed at the makeshift necklace with two cut-off Spock ears dangling from it and pulled on it from behind, choking the man out. Then he grabbed his keys, lazer rifle, and pocket scanner.

Before he could see what the terrorist group ISIS was going to do to other cast members like James Doohan and DeForest Kelley, which the author apparently forgot to write about, he opened a space portal with a small device and ran through it with the keys in his hand. The portal closed and disappeared. No one seemed to have noticed.

But then the portal reappeared and the man ran back out. He went up to the terrorist he had choked out and shot him in the head with a lazer beam. This time *everyone* noticed.

"ALLAHU ACKBAR! JIHAD!!!" ISIS screamed as they started shooting their lazer rifles at the man. A pair of terrorists were especially upset because the man's whole interruption had apparently overshadowed their nefarious slaying of James Doohan and DeForest Kelley, which was really sick and violent and deserved some attention. Instead, some old freak had just appeared to steal their thunder, car keys, and everything.

ISIS was *pissed*.

"GOODBYE, SUCKERS!" the man in the white labcoat shouted. And then he disappeared back through the portal, and the space gate was gone in a flash. It was really sci-fi looking. And with that, the whole scene of mayhem and murder, which included the deaths of the entire original cast of Star Trek by a terrorist group that had apparently traveled there from the future, was over.

CHAPTER TWO
PAPILLON SOO SOO

Whore Alley, Danang, Vietnam, Timedate: July 2nd, 1985

Papillon Soo Soo was not a whore but she would soon be playing one in Stanley Kubrick's new film, *Full Metal Jacket*.

A method actress, Papillon was in Vietnam researching the role by hanging out on the corner with a bunch of local prostitutes, acting all prostitutey. Even though it was the middle of the 80s, Vietnam seemed like it had been untouched by the era. It still felt like it was the 60s and the country had never recovered and moved on since the war. This was perfect since *Full Metal Jacket* was a war movie that took place in 1968.

Papillon was French-Chinese and grew up in England. She did not speak a word of Vietnamese. But that didn't matter; she only needed to study the accent since all of her lines would be in English. She also thought it would help to pick up the body language of the prostitutes as they hung out and tried to attract customers. Even though it was a very small part, it seemed like it was going to be even harder than the work she did in her first film, *A View to a Kill*, the James Bond movie starring Roger Moore and Grace Jones.

The night air felt as hot and humid as the day had been. As she was applying new makeup in the mirror of the alley's nearby bathroom (which also doubled as a *bang room* for johns), she practiced some lines in the mirror in her new accent.

She tried to look seductive.

"Me so horny!" she said, really trying to draw out the line.

It sounded pretty effective.

Nailed it! she thought.

Then she pretended to be talking to an actual john, and tried to look imposing.

"*15 dolla!*" she commanded, hands on her hips.

"Me sucky-sucky! Me love you long time!"

And at that, she started cracking up laughing. It was indeed pretty hilarious. She was sure she was going to give a performance to remember.

She grabbed her purse and turned to leave. She wanted to walk back to the corner and try some of her lines on some guys. Maybe someone would drive by who spoke English, and she could fully interact with them. Papillon smiled at what a professional she was.

She was stopped at the door by a strange man in a white labcoat. He was blocking the door completely and looked *ominous*. Papillon backed away.

"Uh, dude..." she said in her normal accent, kind of like a Valley girl, "I'm not really a hooker, I'm just, like, researching a..."

He lunged at her.

She screamed.

The old man grabbed her and pulled her to the floor and got on top of her. As she struggled, he pulled out a rag and held it against her face until she passed out. Then he used a device to open a very sci-fi-like portal on the bathroom wall and dragged her through it and they both disappeared.

CHAPTER THREE
DERF

Somewhere in South America, Timedate: a Tuesday in the year 90,000 BC

The man emerged from a cave, like some kind of caveman, which is literally what he was. Not like he knew that he was a caveman. He barely knew shit. He was a stupid fucking caveman from some distant era that's not even that interesting because the dinosaurs were already extinct. Because look—if you want cavemen, you can't have dinosaurs. They didn't exist at the same time.

"DERK!" yelled the caveman, and a huge dinosaur-like thing the size of a car came running out of the tree line. It was his pet Glyptodon, a huge, armored, armadillo-like creature who is as extinct as a dinosaur but not one. It flipped over onto its back and the caveman scratched its belly.

"Good Derk," the caveman said, and his pet Glyptodon panted and cooed.

Then the caveman grabbed a nearby human leg bone and threw it, and the massive beast took off after it, running over several of the caveman's neighbors, trampling them to death.

"DERF!" screamed one of the caveman's closest neighbors, a cavewoman that lived in small hut made out of twigs and feces.

She bitched and complained at him in a bunch of words Derf could not understand, so he grabbed his nearby club and bashed her in the head. Once unconsciousness had shut her up, he dragged her by the hair back into his cave and fucked her. It probably wasn't rape, since this was the normal way that cavemen mated. And this book is already starting to seem rapey as it is.

She convulsed and twitched as he raped, I mean, *made love to her*. He had brained her pretty good and her skull was smashed a little and bleeding pretty bad. Derf figured he would just rub some shit in her hair after he was done and it would heal her right up. Why Derf figured this, god only knows.

Christ this is an awful character, a mysterious figure thought as he watched the couple from a nearby spot where he had hidden behind a tree.

Just as Derf orgasmed he thought he saw the big potted plant in the room move a little out the corner of his eye. He had just bought the plant at a local market. They were the new thing and really made his cave look nice. So, it would be terrifying if it were actually full of rats or snakes or something. Derf did not like such small and sneaky creatures.

Anyway, after Derf orgasmed, he rolled over onto to his bear skin rug. He held his lover's hand as she finally stopped twitching, and he sighed, looking at his artwork on the cavern wall.

Derf loved to paint; it was a passion of his. He

believed that lines could be symbols that could become different things, each with their own specific meaning. Some people did not get it, but most people did not understand art anyway.

As Derf admired the cave painting, the tree in the room moved almost fifteen feet towards him. When Derf looked back, it was so close it made him scream, and he shot up off of the floor in a panic. At that moment, a white-haired, white-clothed, wild man jumped out from behind the tree at him. Derf held his hands up in front of his face, too terrified to see what was going to happen next. But the man had run right past him, and when Derf looked again he was gone.

The man in the white clothes came up behind Derf with his club and bashed him over the head.

Derf yelled, "OW!" and reached to touch his head and felt warm blood leaking out. He looked at it on his fingers, dumbfounded.

"Derf?" he asked, and then he fell over, crashing to the ground.

The man aimed his sci-fi device at the ground and opened a portal there. Using his foot, he pushed the caveman into the portal. Derf disappeared like he fell through a hole. The scientist jumped in after him, and the portal disappeared.

The cavewoman woke up and yawned, stretching her arms, and wondered what there was to drink.

"Derf?" she asked. But he was nowhere to be seen.

The cavewoman pouted.

CHAPTER FOUR
GUY MANN

Portland, Oregon, U.S.A., Timedate: April 11th, 2016

Guy stapled a "FREE GREENPEACE" flyer to a pole, wishing his name was something cooler like "Leaf" or "Bud". But not Herb, that sounded like an old hippie's name. Guy wasn't an old hippie. He was a really cool young guy with fresh ideas. He just wished he had a hipper name.

But then he thought, *fuck that, why should I even want a name like that anymore? Now that weed is legal I don't even smoke it. Smoking weed is for conformist hipsters with names like Leaf and Bud.*

Guy adjusted his $200 dollar hipster glasses as he read his flyer. He didn't even need the glasses, but he adjusted them anyway, as if they were going to help him read better.

"FREE GREENPEACE" it said in big green letters.

"As you know, Greenpeace was founded on Earth Day in 1988 by global pioneer Jimmy Carter in an effort to raise awareness on important subjects like trees and peace. But now Greenpeace is in danger. Did you know that 40,000 Greenpeaces become extinct each day? At this rate, soon we will have no trees or peace at all. So, stop and help free a Greenpeace by putting a stop to it once and for all. Call my email address on my Facebook for more details. Guy Mann."

It was probably the best flyer that had ever been hung up in Portland. It looked outstanding with its upside-down pot leaf background, and was printed on 100% recycled paper. Guy assumed that the other flyers were *NOT* printed on 100% recycled paper, so he tore them off the pole, crumpled them up, and threw them in the gutter. Who wanted to go to a reading where they talked about fiction instead of important issues? Who wanted to see one of these terrible bands with horrible names like "Napalm Death" and "Pig Smuggler," who sounded like they obviously hated the environment? Guy thought that kind of negativity did not belong in music. Music should be about trees and peace, while also being green.

"HEY GUY, WHAT THE FUCK ARE YOU DOING?" yelled a baggy-clothed hoodlum from across the street. Guy looked up and asked,

"Are you talking to me?" since his name was Guy and everything.

"OF COURSE I'M TALKING TO YOU, YOU PIECE OF SHIT!"

Guy gasped. His hipster glasses were too expensive to get broken, and this asshole's backwards cap told him he meant business.

"FUCK YOU, ELITIST!" Guy yelled, and

threw his stapler at the man.

It hit him in the chest. The guy got pissed.

"WHAT THE FUCK?!"

Guy yelled effeminately and ran off down the street like a little girl, with the other... *guy* in pursuit. He was short and stubby though, and Guy ran a few miles every day so he was sleek and fast like a gazelle. A gazelle that was green and peaceful.

"YOU TORE DOWN MY FLYERS, YOU PIECE OF SHIT!" the vicious bulldog barked at him, which is what Guy figured his problem with him was. But Guy laughed, because he knew the asshole would never catch up to him. And then Guy could find one of his favorite Portland coffee shops, enjoy a nice IPA pumpkin foamed spiced oyster latte and bum a cigarette off of everybody who walked by for the next few hours while he checked his phone to see who wanted to help him free Greenpeace.

The whole town, probably, Guy thought.

At that moment an old hippie with big white hair clotheslined him from out of nowhere. Guy fell off of his feet backwards onto his back, and smacked his head on the sidewalk. He quickly lost consciousness, thinking, *lame...*

The guy who was going to beat the shit out of Guy arrived just in time to see a mad scientist-looking dude put on a big mirrored visor and shoot a lazer that opened a portal on the sidewalk. The white-haired dude picked up the hipster and slung him over his shoulder easily. Guy was so skinny he must've only weighed 125 pounds. The pair walked through the portal and disappeared, and it closed leaving tracers of blue and pink electric sparks.

"DUDE!" the guy shouted. "THAT WAS SCI-FI AS FUCK!"

CHAPTER FIVE
NIGEL DICKINSON

London, England, U.K., Timedate: 31st of August, 1997

Nigel Dickinson was proud of himself. He had fucked the most halfway-decent looking girl from the bar last night. Well, he had technically *shagged* her since he was very, very British and that was the correct term for fucking someone. He had reeled her in with his handsome good looks and charm (he was almost as good looking as Hugh Grant), and then dazzled her with his Oxford College education. He said smart things like, *"I've read a lot of books,"* and *"I know the exchange rate of currency,"* because *"I use the metric system."* She was so impressed that she went home with him in his expensive Ferrari to his big mansion.

But now it was morning, and she needed to go. See, that wasn't actually his car. And this was not his mansion. Nigel Dickinson was merely a butler, and his master, who was probably that guy who narrated *The Lifestyles of the Rich and Famous,* or someone equally British, had been out of town on business for the evening. But he would be arriving home later that morning. So,

Nigel's temporary house guest had to go.

"Fancy some tea?" Nigel asked, entering the room with a tray of tea and crumpets, as if she wasn't going to have a choice.

But she was sitting on the bed surrounded by crumpled up tissues, sobbing as she watched the TV.

"PRINCESS DIANA IS DEAD!!!" she wailed.

"Oh dear..." Nigel responded, meaning to say her name, which he could not recall at the moment. He had a dilemma. He did not have time to console her.

She sniffled.

"She was the most beautiful Princess in the whole world, and now she's dead. When I was a little girl, Princess Di visited my family's village and threw roses at our cottage door. I always wondered why a Princess would visit and toss flowers at our door, but that was just the kind of person she was."

Nigel thought she was making no sense. That sounded like the stupidest thing he'd ever heard. And didn't she know the Princess was slowly dying for the last few days anyway? Didn't she know about the big accident she was in? Nigel was *glad* she finally died. Everyone was making such a big deal out of it you would think the *Queen herself* was in a horrible drunk driving accident.

And "Princess" Diana wasn't even royalty anymore, so who cared? It annoyed the shit out of him.

Nigel thought there was no point in having this conversation with her, so he decided to kick her out. He put down the tea tray, and went to get her out of his boss's bed.

"Alright now," he said. "Off you go."

She gave him a ferocious stare that said, *do not touch*.

"Are you having me on?" she asked.

"No, absolutely not, very sad about her highness, the whore, now bugger off."

The girl gasped, trying to find the right words to throw back at him.

"You... you... you..." she repeated, "you *unpatriotic, impolite* BASTARD!"

"And you're a rude bitch, now toodle-pip!"

"And you have a small penis! That was the smallest one I've ever seen! It was like being fucked by NOTHING!"

Nigel gasped. He had a major complex about his very small penis. He thought he more than made up for it with his good looks and charm.

"It is perfectly average, thank you very much!"

"Yeah, if average were *TWO INCHES!*"

"You don't even understand the metric system! That's like, *SIX INCHES* in our country!"

"THAT DOESN'T EVEN MAKE ANY SENSE!" she screamed, and before he knew it, she was attacking him like an angry witch, trying to scratch his eyes out.

"PISS OFF, YOU ANGRY WITCH!" he screamed.

And then he heard his boss pulling up in the driveway in his stretch limo.

"Bloody hell, my boss is coming!"

"Your *BOSS?!*" she screamed.

"Yes, my boss! I'm just a butler! I just work here! Now get off me, you angry witch!"

Nigel raised his hand as if to smack her but, luckily, her head suddenly exploded when a violent lazer blast shot her from across the room.

Oh thank god, Nigel thought. *I can't believe I almost struck a woman.*

He wiped her blood out of his eyes and looked at the figure standing in the doorway, thinking it was his boss. He just figured his boss was rich enough to afford such a thing as a lazer gun and hated unwanted houseguests. Nigel's mind reeled at what his punishment would be.

But it wasn't his boss. It was an old man wearing a white labcoat, holding what was apparently a lazer rifle, and looking generally all futuristic. The man seemed to be fumbling with the settings on the weapon.

"Who...?" Nigel started to ask, but was cut off by a sudden lazer blast to the chest. He was knocked to the floor, stunned. As he lost consciousness, he remembered an old television show from his childhood that this reminded him of. It only lasted for one season though. But for the life of him he could not remember what it was called. Then he passed out.

The man in the lab coat once again dragged a man through what you can correctly assume is some kind of time portal. Before it disappeared, he briefly came back to grab the tray of tea and crumpets. Then he was gone.

CHAPTER SIX
TZARCYZK-616

Clipton-Nik 5, The Vesta Galaxy, Timedate:
Negative-26371264 Alpha 80

Nervous and excited, Tzarcyzk-616 punched the coordinates into his timepod's computer.

APRIL 11TH, 2016, PORTLAND, OREGON, U.S.A., PLANET EARTH

He flipped the switch, and time and space warped around him, sending him hurtling back to the past of a different world.

Tzarcyzk gripped his "Free Greenpeace" flyer, reading it over and over again with excitement. He had been in contact with the man who left his name on the flyer via timephone, and was very concerned about the plight of his people, vowing to stop everything and help him. Luckily, Tzarcyzk-616 pretty much looked human, or... enough that he could blend in. In a town like Portland it was unlikely that anyone would notice his ears and nose were slightly different, or his fingers were slightly longer, or two springy stalks grew out of his head with glittery star-shaped appendages attached to them. He would probably fit in just fine.

Tzarcyzk-616 briefly went over a few of his note cards. He had them prepared for almost any given situation, and tried to memorize them. They were simple phrases in the local native language that would hopefully help him to fit in and communicate peacefully with the people.

The timepod landed at its destination, and Tzarcyzk-616 gathered his things into his pack and eagerly jumped out to explore.

Portland, Oregon was a fiery wasteland of volcanic ash and bubbly lava. The air sizzled around him, so sulfuric he could barely breathe. In the distance Tzarcyzk could see a great silver pyramid with a glaring red eye at the peak. It fixed its gaze in Tzarcyzk's direction and a siren blared as a deep and distance voice spoke.

"FREEEEEE...GREEEEEEN... PEEEEEE-ACE ..." it grumbled.

A huge lazer suddenly shot out of the eye and hit a volcano, which exploded. The sirens continued.

"FREEEEEE...GREEEEEEN... PEEEEEE-ACE.." it moaned once more. A gate at the base of the pyramid opened and out poured thousands of giant flying robots, all of them propelled by rocket fire and shooting lazer beams from their eyes and mouths.

The cacophony of lazers and explosions were deafening and the nightmarish scene entranced Tzarcyzk-616. It was almost like the eye had fixated on him and held him in place. But then he remembered the *Free Will* app on his watch and pressed it.

But he pressed *Free Wi-Fi* instead, and the internet connected on his watch and a video message started repeating on a loop, "This is hell! We've created hell! You shouldn't have listened to us! Why? WHY?!?" The man on the screen looked very panicked and was bleeding from his eyes, ears, and mouth as he frantically scratched off his own face with his fingers.

Tzarcyzk-616 shut off the free Wi-Fi via voice command and turned the Free Will on instead. This allowed him to jump out of the way of a gigantic red lazer beam just in time to not be obliterated by it. He ran back to the safety of his ship and shut the door. As he tried to catch his breath, he noticed the timedate on the control console. It wasn't April 11th, 2016, it was April 11th, *2026*. That explained everything. Tzarcyzk-616 had arrived ten years too late, and because of his miscalculation, he was unable to help out and this led to the destruction of Portland. He cursed himself for not being good enough to stop the end of the world. If only he had taken more classes in college, this probably wouldn't have happened.

As he checked his watch to see if there was an app for relieving depression available, he heard a knock on the outside door of his timepod. He pressed a button to make the door translucent and noticed a man outside in full protective radioactive gear. Thinking he must be a survivor in need of his help, Tzarcyzk-616 opened the door of his spacepod to let the man in. And in he came, removing his airtight helmet to reveal his shock of white hair and his excited grin.

"Hello," the man said. "You're my first alien."

Tzarcyzk fumbled for his note cards to find the correct response to the man, but it was too late. The pod filled with a noxious gas that made him fall right asleep.

Besides, even if he had made a card that said, *'Please do not knock me out and abduct me, I am a friendly alien,'* it wouldn't have helped anyway.

The old man, who we can only assume is some kind of time scientist at this point, abducting people for some kind of experiment, took over the controls and flew the timepod away into the unknown, wherever that is.

(You'll find out later.)

CHAPTER SEVEN
FRANKENSTEIN

Auschwitz, Germany, Timedate: the 24th of December, Christmas Eve, 1942

We all know the classic tale. Dr. Frankenstein creates a green-skinned monstrosity, and it comes to life only to be thrown in a concentration camp for its Jewish last name. Some would say the monster was actually Dr. Frankenstein himself, and the monster of his creation did not deserve to be called by his last name as well. But the monster was anyway, since it was Nazi Germany during World War II and the name Frankenstein sounded very, very Jewy. It also did not help that the monster said the name everywhere it went, *"FRANKENSTEIN, RAAA!"* and tried to sell people gold watches. The monster would roll up his sleeve, and there would be several glimmering timepieces. He was always ready to make a deal.

So, for being a street peddler with a Jewish name, and not being registered, Frankenstein's Monster was captured by Nazi soldiers. Even though the monster was quite fearsome, and strong, he quickly cowered before their flamethrowers, terrified of the burning fire.

Frankenstein had spent a long winter in the Auschwitz concentration camp. He was shunned by the Jews for being a monster and tortured by the guards for being Jewish. The only friends he made were the ones he stitched together from random body parts. He worked as a *sonderkommando*, shoveling dead Jews into the ovens, so he always had the best pieces to choose from. Once he had the perfect makeshift friend put together, he would drag it outside and throw it as hard as he could against the electric fence surrounding the camp, and the high voltage electricity would course through the body and bring it to life. Soon, Frankenstein had an army of super-strong dead Jew monsters at his command, and they eventually destroyed all of the Nazis and took over the camp. There was a lot of scary fire in their way at first, as the soldiers utilized their flamethrowers, but the monsters overwhelmed them with sheer numbers and brute strength.

That morning, as the fires burned out, it snowed. Frankenstein observed the camp from a nearby hilltop with a heavy heart. He did not know where he would go next, or what he would do. Should he try to find his creator? Track down Hitler? Lead his people to a new paradise? He did not want to do any of these things.

Then a small child approached Frankenstein with a gift wrapped in satin.

"Merry Christmas, Frankenstein! Thank you for saving us. Take this as a token of our appreciation."

She smiled and ran off.

Frankenstein had never gotten a Christmas present before. Hell, this was his first Christmas. Suddenly excited, he unwrapped his gift.

It was a beautiful gold watch that looked like it was worth a lot of money. And it was inscribed on the back. Frankenstein had learned to read at camp with a diary written by a young girl named Anne Frank. The inscription read, "Frankenstein Forever."

Frankenstein smiled. The sentiment made his heart swell. And he knew what he wanted to do now. He wanted to open a jewelry store, one that sold the finest gold watches and other high-end accessories. It would be the best store in all of Germany. And nothing was going to stand in his way. Frankenstein stood up, ready to walk into his future.

An old man with white hair and a long white laboratory coat stood in his way, looking like some kind of sadistic Nazi scientist.

Frankenstein growled at him, "GRRRRRR!" and rushed to attack the man. But it was already too late. A portal opened right in front of the lumbering beast and he disappeared into it. The man shot lazer beams into the portal as he followed him in. You could hear the screams of the monster and a loud thud before the portal closed, if you were listening.

But no one was listening. Frankenstein's war had ended. And another one was about to begin.

CHAPTER EIGHT
PAUL

Hammerfest, Norway, Timedate: January 1st, 1000 AD, 8AM

Paul had fucked so many Swedish whores last night that his dick hurt. But what can you do when you're the biggest hunk in Norway? You bang a lot of whores.

The night before had been one hell of a party. For years everyone had prophesied that *Ragnarök* would come at midnight, destroying the world and sending everyone straight to Valhalla. Scholars were even calling it "Y1K". So, whether it was going to happen or not, everyone decided to throw a party to end all parties. It had been a good millennium, and if there was to be a new one, that would be good too. Warring tribes had even stopped fighting and banded together to party on what might have been their final night.

Hence Paul fucking so many Swedish whores. His people had been at war with the Swedes for a long time. He didn't even really know why. He had spent so much of his life drinking and killing and fucking that he never stopped to ask any questions. But now he was wondering, as he basked in the glow of this wonderful new millennium morning, what if? Why? And how?! There must be more to life than this. There must be a place beyond the stars, more real than Valhalla. And now that the next millennium had arrived and he had lived to see it, who knows what the future could bring? Why bother to continue conquering the lands when he could conquer the stars? Why settle for the world when he could have worlds beyond? Maybe fuck some different women, see what that's like. All sorts of things.

But Paul was just your typical Viking. A strong warrior, skilled with an axe and a sword. Typically tall, maybe a bit taller than all of his brothers, but just as tall as the average Scandinavian man. He had long blond hair and a red beard. He did not stick out too much. He just looked like everyone else did. And Vikings looked a bit less barbaric these days and a bit more well dressed. After all, it was the year 1000 now. It was the future. Advances in metalworking had made them look like they were straight from Valhalla. Vikings were futuristically shiny now and had cooler weapons.

His life had been full. He had traveled the seas near and far. Found riches and lived well. He had loved many a beautiful woman and, even though he would never admit it, a few men as well. Sometimes all at the same time. He was an expert swordsman and tales of his sword reached far and wide. His sword was named Gigantica, and Paul liked to boast it was almost as big as his penis. And through it all, he had seen many a battle and lived through them without any scars to tell the story.

But his story here was ending. Paul wondered if it were written, would it be interesting enough? He had not done anything that had not been done before, been anywhere no one had ever been, seen things no one had ever seen. He would be forgotten by time. Maybe he would have been better off if Ragnarök had come. There was nothing else that could be done here. Nothing new. No new opportunities. Everything would stay the same as it ever was. He prayed to Odin that it would not always be like this.

Then, at that moment, a light show unlike any other he had ever seen erupted in the nearby dell. *Well,* he thought, *that's a start.*

A man appeared on the glade unlike any other. His silvery visor glinted in the morning sun, making him appear to be a specter of light. His white shock of hair was almost invisible. His long white coat flapped in the breeze. He wielded what appeared to be a large metal club.

"SURTUR!" a Viking gasped, probably thinking the man was some villain from Norse mythology.

The man in the labcoat clutched his weapon, and it glowed red.

"ATTACK!" the Viking screamed, and rose to attack the man, drawing his sword.

A blinding blast of light shot out of the man's weapon and punched a hole clean through the warrior. Paul could see through the gaping hole, and the Viking fell.

"NOOO!" Paul screamed.

With a weapon like that, their swords and spears and axes would be useless. Paul watched in horror as his brothers rushed in to attack.

"DON'T!" he yelled, as if in slow-mo.

His brothers were mowed down left and right by bright red light, which made a sound like lightning each time it shot through the air. Norsemen fell, slaughtered. This was no epic battle—it was a massacre.

Paul did not attack. He remained standing, frozen still. When the smoke cleared, all he asked was, "WHY?"

The man in the white coat walked towards him, and spoke.

"THEY WERE COMING STRAIGHT AT ME! I WAS ONLY DEFENDING MYSELF!"

Paul did not understand his language but he sounded foreign.

Then the man lowered his glasses, and said in Norwegian, "Hi, Paul."

His weapon glowed blue and he shot a bright blue lazer blast at Paul. Paul blocked it with his shield.

The man said, "Oh shit."

Paul the Viking rushed him, tackling the old man and sending them both flying backwards through the air. The white-haired man pressed a button on the device on his wrist and a portal opened, and they both went through it.

They landed with a thud on a shiny metal floor in a big shiny metal room. Paul let the old man go and stood up and looked at his surroundings, mouth agape in complete shock. Several people, some looking quite odd, looked back at him. Some looked friendly, some didn't. The man in the white laboratory coat got up off the ground and dusted himself off and readdressed the Viking.

"Paul," he said, "Please allow me to introduce myself. I am Y, and I come from your distant future. I have gathered you here," he paused for a second, looking around the room, "*all* of you... for a purpose."

"And what purpose is that?" asked someone who sounded entirely too British.

"For the purpose of science."

Paul had no idea what that was, but it sounded ominous.

CHAPTER NINE
CAPTURED

They all started freaking out pretty quickly.

"Where the hell are we, man?" Guy asked no one in general.

Nigel answered, in his thick British accent, "I think we're on some sort of spaceship, like on that show *Star Trek* or something."

"What?! I can't understand a word you're saying! And is that Frankenstein's Monster, for fucksake?" Guy said, pointing to Frankenstein's Monster.

"Frankenstein, *RAAAAA!*" the monster replied.

"Is this an audition?" asked Papillon.

Everyone started talking at once.

"SILENCE!" Y shouted, and he snapped his fingers.

Seven metal chambers suddenly shot out of the floor underneath each person, grabbing them with flexing coils and stretching their arms and legs apart and holding them in place. The structure clicked and whirred around them, metal parts moving at menacing speeds with blinking red and blue lights, saw blades, needles, pincers, and wires. Metal hooks from spider-like appendages held open their eyelids and mouths. They couldn't close their eyes or even scream. It was all very terrifying.

"Now," said Y, "I hope that was as confusing as it would be hard to describe if someone had to."

Tzarcyzk-616 tried to nod. Even if he had written everything down that just happened, it would probably be impossible to relay that to someone. It was just so complicated. Like you had to be there.

The man in the white labcoat walked around surveying his captives in their torture chamber-like devices like they were just test subjects to do whatever he wanted with.

"Like I was saying, I have gathered you all here for a purpose," he said, addressing the whole room.

"My name is Doctor Yes. But you can just call me Y. You are currently being injected with a serum that will make you all understand each other's languages, dialects, and accents, so there will be no confusion during your interactions. I want you to work as a team."

Doctor Yes said that last part while looking directly at Guy, as if he needed to hear it the most.

"You will be given this ship to command. You are in deep space, in the distant future."

Tzarcyzk-616 felt like raising his hand to tell the Doctor that he was already from the distant future, not 2026 like where he found him. He wondered if the Doctor already knew that, but he was much more curious about whether he was in an even more distant future, because if so, that would be exciting.

"You are all from different points in time. Now,

before I tell you what your mission is, I would like to go around the room and have everyone state their name and where they're from, so you can start getting to know each other."

The restraints receded from their faces.

"Let's start with you," Doctor Yes motioned towards Nigel.

"Uh, OK..." Nigel said, a little bit nervous. "My name is Nigel Dickinson, and I am from London, England. The year 1997."

Then he tried to smile a bit and said, "Cheers!"

Everyone could totally understand him this time.

"Next," said the Doctor, pointing to Paul.

Paul sneered at him and, gritting his teeth, he said, "I'm Paul. I'm from Norway and I come from the year 1-2-Fuck-You."

"Relax," said the Doctor, and he pressed a button on his wrist pad and everyone was injected with a relaxing agent.

Everyone relaxed a little more.

"Next!"

The green-skinned monster responded almost gently.

"Frankenstein. Raaa."

The caveman felt like saying that too. He smiled and said, "Derf. *Raaa.*"

"And if you are all wondering, Frankenstein is from Germany in the 1940s and Derf is from 90,000 BC, somewhere in South America. He is what some of you might know as a caveman," the Doctor noted.

Paul did not know cavemen. He thought it was bullshit.

"Next," the Doctor said, pointing to Papillon.

She started remembering their first encounter and wondered if she should stay in character.

She decided to go for it, and responded in a heavy Vietnamese accent.

"Me Soo Soo, baby. Me so horny. Me love you long time." She turned to Paul and asked, "You got girlfriend?"

Paul smiled at her. He suddenly wanted to fuck her so bad. And he was sure it was going to happen sooner or later. He was excited. He couldn't wait to get out of this torture chamber and start the experiment the Doctor wanted to do on them. He didn't even care what it was. He was sure it was going to be fun.

Unbeknownst to a lot of them, a chemical agent was being injected into their bloodstream that was making them forget certain parts of their memories. Like, for instance, Paul had just forgotten completely how the Doctor slaughtered his people. Soo Soo just forgot the Doctor was the menacing character in the bathroom who she thought was going to rape and kill her. Nigel forgot he had a really small penis, even though he would unfortunately find out that was still true later.

But the chemical was being used for the most part to make them more trusting of the Doctor. This would make them all more willing to help him out with his experiment.

"I'm Guy Mann and I'm a Portland hipster from the year 2016," said Guy, being completely honest.

Everyone kind of heard him say his introduction as, "I'm a guy, man." which seemed too general. But people were OK with it.

"Does anyone have any drugs?" he asked.

He looked over at Soo Soo.

"You seem like the kind of girl that likes to party," he told her.

Soo Soo remembered one of her lines that would be applicable to the situation.

"Anytin you want, baby."

"That brings up my next point, and now that everyone knows each other, we can get started."

"*But...*" Tzarcyzk-616 almost said, having been totally skipped over. Did anyone even care? Probably not, so he decided it was right to not even speak up. He thought his intro would probably be more interesting than, say, *Frankenstein's*, and it might have even made him a little popular if people knew where he was actually from. But, they wouldn't get the chance. And now no one would probably like him, ever.

Tzarcyzk-616 frowned with sadness.

Doctor Yes continued, "I am going to inject you all with a hallucinogenic drug called LSD, or acid, as it is more commonly known in my era. I'm from the 1960s, by the way, in case I didn't say when I introduced myself."

"*Alright!*" Guy said, all excited. LSD was his new favorite drug. Ever since he quit smoking weed, it was the only thing he indulged in. And since it was still highly illegal in Portland, unlike weed, there was more of a danger to using it. It was a Schedule 1 drug, according to the law, right up there with such hardcore things as heroin. It carried with it a penalty of not upwards of a five thousand dollar fine and two years in prison.

It was the best drug ever.

Nigel Dickinson was also aware of this, and it terrified him. The main reason he would never do drugs is the fear of getting caught. He immediately imagined going to prison for trying acid just once. He would be caught on his first try, making the experience even more terrible. He would subsequently be raped in prison by big fat hairy men on a daily basis, and then every girlfriend he ever had would be brought in one by one to make fun of his small penis.

Dropping acid seemed like his worst nightmare.

Papillon was not actually into the idea but didn't want to break character.

Tzarcyzk-616 figured he was probably immune to the effects of such a drug because of his alien biology. And if anything, he might have a different reaction to it than everyone else.

Paul, Derf, and Frankenstein did not really know what the Doctor was talking about.

Paul was kind of excited though—he just simply could not stop being excited about anything that could be coming up next! He was ready to prove that he probably wasn't a boring stereotypical character. He was sure he could prove to himself and everyone else that there might actually be more to a Viking than history would think.

He did not doubt himself.

Derf missed his pet Glyptodon, Derk.

Frankenstein did not know what acid was either, but it sounded bad. One time, Hitler gave him crystal meth and he went on a three day rampage destroying tanks and killing both Russian and German soldiers in a murderous frenzy. He remembered coming down off it was really rough and it made him very sad to see what he had done. He hated Hitler. He was such a bad person.

"You are being injected with a small dose at first. Your next doses will be a larger amount just in case you build a bit of a tolerance to it. You also will not remember everything that just happened exactly, but you *will* know each other and have the knowledge of where you are. There will be a bit of extra knowledge added to make you more comfortable with your surroundings and what you are doing on the ship."

With the injection of LSD into their bloodstreams, the needles retracted. And then the mechanical chambers that were holding everyone in place folded back into themselves and retreated into the floor from where they came. They all stretched and positioned themselves on the cool metallic ground again, also still feeling the relaxation agent.

The Doctor had a stack of clothes in his arms that he started handing out. They were specific to each person and were different colors, but some had the same color.

"These are your uniforms. Please put them on."

Everyone started looking at their uniforms curiously, kind of excited as if they were a nice gift.

"And this is your ship. It is called the S.S. Mashrue." The Doctor motioned in general to their complete surroundings.

"Explore, and find the bridge. There will be instructions waiting there. I might see you again later."

He waved goodbye and said, "Good luck."

Papillon Soo Soo stopped looking at her elegant and futuristic blue jumpsuit for a second to see a strange man disappear through a fascinating set of doors that opened and closed as if by magic. He had fuzzy white hair and a long, white coat that seemed to follow behind him like a tail.

She felt compelled to follow the mystery man and catch him, just to see what he was all about.

She had a feeling she was about to enter a whole world of wonder.

CHAPTER TEN
S.S. MASHRUE

The time-displaced test subjects put on their uniforms. All were the same design but different colors.

"Hmmm..." Nigel thought out loud. "This is *also* like that obscure sci-fi show from the 60s. The *Star Trek* or something. Each crew member had a different coloured uniform and it stood for their rank."

"Sounds pretty lame," said Guy. "No one cares about that retro crap anymore. It's so out of style."

"I think it looks cool," Paul disagreed. "Don't you think so, Soo Soo?"

Soo Soo looked at herself in her tight blue outfit, admiring her arms and legs in them.

"Ooooh," she responded, "It make me *so horny!*"

"So, then we're a crew," Paul looked back at Nigel to confirm this. "And as a Viking, I've commanded many a crew on a longship. I've led my men into battle, I've led my men during expeditions to explore, and for trips out for basic pleasure. So, I'm obviously the natural born leader, whatever this color stands for."

Nigel looked at Paul's uniform. It was green.

"I do not remember any green coloured uniforms

from the show. They were only blue, red, and a yellow or beige colour. Hard to describe," Nigel said, wondering if he should be putting the U sound into the word colour when he said it, but then wondered why he thought that, since spelling and speaking are obviously not the same thing. But now he couldn't get $U's$ out of his head, and wondered about Z. He knew that words like "lazer" definitely have a Z in it when you say them. Not an S instead of a Z. *That would be ludicrous,* he thought, using a word in his head with a U and an S in it that could maybe go either way!

Nigel was tripping out.

"But my uniform is also green," Guy said. "Green is definitely a leader's color. I come from a city where we are *very* green. And it means we're the best. Keep Oregon Green, is the saying."

Or is it Keep Oregon Clean... Guy wondered. *That's weird, I should know. Portland is weird...*

"Anyway, my uniform is green, and I'm the smartest person here anyway because I'm from the furthest year in the future."

Tzarcyzk almost spoke up to interject that *he* was actually the person from the furthest year away in the future, but decided it was probably not in his best interest to get in an argument with Guy. He seemed very assertive.

"So, I'm obviously leader, not Paul."

But Paul didn't object because he was busy talking to Soo Soo and wasn't even paying attention.

"Blue looks pretty good on you, babe. You're as beautiful as the steam rising from the spilled innards of a thousand slain foes on an icy field," he told her. This line had gotten his dick wet in many lands.

Nigel cleared his throat.

"In any case, if I remember correctly, the yellowish-beige colour was actually the colour of the captain, and of the helmsmen. Any science officer or doctor had a blue-coloured uniform," he said, seeing the British letters in his words as he spoke them again, "and red was more for engineers or security officers. Basically the muscle."

"For instance," Nigel continued, "Frankenstein and our young caveman friend have red uniforms. So I would say that Frankenstein would be our head of security and Derf would be the engineer."

"Frankenstein. *Strong,*" Frankenstein replied, holding up his arms so everyone could see his bulging biceps.

Derf immediately mimicked this.

"Derf strong too. And *smart.*"

Frankenstein sneered a little and said, "*Frankenstein smart!*"

"Derf smart *more.* Derf make ship *go.*"

Derf motioned with his hands, as if he were going to make the ship fly.

"*RAAA!*" yelled Frankenstein.

"OK, break it up, you two." Paul got between them before it got physical.

"Spoken like a true captain," Nigel said.

"HEY!" Guy disagreed.

"And I'm in a blue uniform, as is young Ms. Soo Soo, which you look quite *posh* in, by the way," he winked at her.

"Tank you!" she replied.

"So, I would assume the role of intelligence officer, which is basically the captain's right hand man, or his number one in charge, if you will."

"Sounds good to me," Paul agreed. "You *do* sound like the smartest man here."

"HEY!" Guy yelled again.

"And Ms. Soo Soo will obviously do well as the ship's doctor, or counselor. Can you do that for us, baby?" Nigel asked.

"Anytin you want!" she agreed.

Papillon actually took a course in psychiatry in college, and even though she got more into New Age and spiritual stuff later on in school, it was still a subject she was interested in.

Then she wondered why she was still in character as a Vietnamese prostitute and remembered her acting coach snapping at her about never breaking character. She also wondered if that was even applicable to this situation and then suddenly remembered she should be chasing a mysterious rabbit through the door.

"Me so horny! We get out a here, or what?" she pointed towards the doors of the big bay room I forgot to mention they were in.

"In a minute, Counselor Soo," Nigel said.

"You," he pointed at Tzarcyzk-616, "in the

beige-yellow shirt. Who might you be, again?"

"My name is Tzarc—"

Nigel cut him off.

"Jolly good, Zarsh. You are the pilot. If you do not know how to fly this ship I'm sure you can learn how."

Tzarcyzk-616 was more than confident he could fly a starship, no matter what kind it was. He was less confident, however, in his communication skills and worried about even attempting to be part of a team. Maybe, if he got some alone time with Counselor Soo, she might be able to help him with that.

Nigel clapped his hands together.

"Alright team, then let's go Star Trekking! Captain?"

"Oh," Paul said, "Yes, everyone follow me. I will lead us straight to the helm and into adventure beyond your wildest dreams!"

Does he really just say things like that? Tzarcyzk wondered. *It seems so rehearsed and like he doesn't even need note cards. It just seems to come flying out of his mouth, whatever nonsense he wants to say. I wish I could be more like that.*

Tzarcyzk was eager to follow the Viking and was now more fixated on observing him. Paul could be someone he could learn a lot from.

But when Guy complained again about Paul taking command, Tzarcyzk-616 suddenly realized something he couldn't believe he'd missed before. He must need to be rebooted if he didn't notice this huge minor detail sticking out right in front of him:

That whiny hipster was Guy Mann, whom he had communicated with about his flyer, Free Greenpeace.

It was mindblowing. What a coincidence. It was such a coincidence that it couldn't just be a coincidence. Tzarcyzk would have to introduce himself soon but suddenly felt more anxious and nervous than he ever had before.

When everyone followed Paul as a group, a set of doors suddenly slid open and retreated into the walls all futuristically, leaving a big entrance.

"*WOAH!!!*" the whole crew exclaimed at once.

That really tripped everyone the fuck out.

CHAPTER ELEVEN
THE LSD TAKES HOLD

The spaceship was a bit much. It would have overwhelmed most of them in the first place, being so futuristic and all, but as the acid took hold it was another matter entirely. It was vast, shiny, and labyrinthine. Light beamed down hallways that seemed to stretch on forever. Strange space sounds clicked and whirred in the distance, echoing through the corridors. You couldn't tell whether they were coming from far away or were going off nearby.

"How are we going to find the bridge?" Paul asked. "It's just a bunch of shiny corridors that seem to go on and on forever."

Tzarcyzk-616 knew the answer. He had been aboard starships just like this one before. It was as simple as finding the lift. The bridge was usually on the top floor. A control panel on the nearby wall would probably show the way.

But before he could tell him, Paul told Nigel, "Number One! You're my first officer. Now tell me the way to the ship's control center."

"Do you hear music?" Nigel asked, looking into the distance.

"Number One!" Paul snapped. "Snap out of it!"

Nigel snapped out of it, but then was thrown

off for a minute.

Is a gigantic, red-bearded Viking talking to me? Nigel wondered. *He looks like a relic of a lost time. Blimey! And is that Frankenstein? Frankenstein is supposed to be fictional. What the bloody hell is going on?!*

"Uh..." Nigel answered.

"WAIT!" Paul held up his hand to shush him.

"I hear it too. It sounds like a beer festival is in town for *midvinter*."

Tzarcyzk-616 started writing a message down on one of his note cards. He clicked his pen and it scared the shit out of Frankenstein.

"RAAAA!" Frankenstein shouted, throwing his hands up in the air.

"BY ODIN'S BEARD!" Paul yelled. "DOES ANYBODY ELSE SEE THAT THING!?"

Tzarcyzk-616 handed Nigel a note card.

It read: *On the wall behind you is a touchscreen control panel. Just tap it to turn it on. You will see a map and the closest ~~elevator~~ lift will be shown somewhere on it. It will probably go to the bridge.*

After Nigel read the card, he looked at Tzarcyzk-616's face. It was looking really alien. The ears seemed to be getting longer and the eyes looked like they were getting wider. The whole face looked like it was morphing. Nigel gasped, and then he started backing away from the boy with his eyes still fixed on him.

He ended up bumping into the wall panel and a computer screen lit up in front of them. It booted up and a video message started playing.

It was a man in strange-looking ceremonial garb.

He spoke, "I and my musicians are musical astronauts. We sail the galaxies through the medium of sound, and take our audiences with us whether they want to go or not. The audience might want to be earth bound, but we being space bound we bind them to us and thus they cannot resist because the space way is the better way to travel. It keeps going out, and out, and further out than that."

The message froze. Everyone was in awe. It tripped Nigel out the most though.

"Was that... *Sun Ra?*" he asked no one in particular.

"Sun Ra?" Paul scoffed, and said, "This sounds like the name of a demon."

"He was only one of the most important jazz musicians of all time," Guy rolled his eyes at Paul. "Geez, everyone has heard of him. I have the import of his *Live in Keetmanshoop* on colored vinyl."

Guy completely ignored the fact that Paul could not have ever heard of him because he hadn't even been born yet. But he was so sick of Paul's shit, anyway. If he wasn't so tough looking he would probably kick his ass. The Viking better not tell him what to do again, or else.

"Yeah, it's Sun Ra," Nigel nodded. "The message is from an old movie he did called *Space is the Place*. It's from the 60s, I think. Kind of fitting, isn't it?"

"Make him speak again," Paul said, just basically delighted to be seeing something such as a television.

"OK, let me try to unwhack it."

Nigel smacked the screen with his hand. The channel changed.

"ALLAHU ACKBAR!" a bunch of men holding large swords screamed.

Everyone gasped.

A bunch of wavy unreadable letters were on the screen. The only ones that you could read were "The Al-Jazeera Network".

They kept violently screaming and ululating. One of them pushed a blindfolded man to the ground and started cutting through his neck with a knife until his head was severed completely. He held it up and screamed, "JIHAD! JIHAD!"

Everyone screamed.

"Turn it off! Turn it off!" Nigel yelled, even though he was the one who had turned it on.

Paul had seen a lot of violence in his life, but never by any men like that.

"Who were they?" he asked.

"That's ISIS," Guy responded. "They're a terrorist group from my time. One of the reasons I started Free Greenpeace was to stop radical groups like that. I actually need to post one of their videos like that online to raise awareness. But I've been really busy lately."

Guy didn't really feel anything yet, and it was obvious the other guys were, so he was starting to think he got really bunk acid. He suddenly thought it was probably a conspiracy against him. And he was going to do something about it the first chance he got.

"Anyway," he went on instead, "this is kind of a clusterfuck here. Will someone please open the goddamn door to the elevator so we can get on with it?"

"Fine, lad," Nigel responded. "Don't go off your trolley."

Nigel found the button to the lift on the touchscreen and pressed it. The doors automatically opened. The controls were right in front of them the whole time.

"After you, your majesty," Nigel gestured to Guy.

Guy started to walk in, but Paul pushed him out of the way and said, "Captain first."

"HEY!" Guy whined.

And when he tried to follow right behind him, Nigel stopped him.

"First officer second."

This pissed Guy off even more. But he went right along, followed by Tzarcyzk-616 and Frankenstein. Three guys, an alien, and a monster from World War II. It seemed like the incorrect number of people.

Nigel hit the button for the top floor on the lift and they went up anyway.

Frankenstein screamed so much they had to hold him back so he wouldn't destroy all of the controls.

CHAPTER TWELVE
THE BRIDGE

Tzarcyzk-616 had been the only one to note that there were people in the group who were also not talking as much as he was, because they simply were not there. Counselor Soo and Derf the Caveman were nowhere to be seen and seemed to have been forgotten about completely. He meant to bring it up but figured he should follow the leader. But it would be important to know where they went. Derf could have knocked her out and dragged her away to be raped for all they knew. Raped in some kind of kinky sex room. He was sure the ship had one. These kinds of starships always did.

But no, when they got to the bridge, Papillon Soo Soo was sitting there in a chair doing her nails, and Derf was at a console playing some kind of video game and drooling.

"Wow, I forgot those two existed," Guy said, dismissively. He didn't really give a fuck about anyone else, especially not some Asian whore and a caveman.

"How did you two get up here?" Nigel asked them.

Derf made a hand gesture like a door opening and then pointed up through it.

"Derf and Soo Soo go."

"Are you two hooking up or something?" Paul asked.

Soo Soo shook her head, thinking of an excuse.

"No, Derf got girlfriend back home. No sucky-sucky."

As if, Papillon thought. *Gag me with a spoon.*

"Nigel," Derf grunted. "Come. Use eyes."

Nigel followed Derf over to the console. It was covered in different symbols and odd alien writing.

"Derf know. Look."

He pressed a button and the whole wall opened up before them like a window, displaying the spectacular view of outer space right in front of them.

Nigel was astonished.

"Lovely, mate! Bloody spectacular!"

"Yeah, maybe he's not so useless after all," Guy said.

"Of course not! Our friendly caveman is more like a Fred Flintstone-type. As a matter of fact, I think we should just call him Fred from now on. Would you like that, Fred?" Nigel asked the caveman.

"Derf Fred," he agreed.

"Splendid!" Nigel exclaimed.

(His mind would break later when he realized Fred was Derf spelled backwards.)

"Now, what else can this ship do, Fred, my dear lad?" Nigel asked.

"Derf make ship go," the caveman said, apparently already forgetting about his new name.

He pressed a button and the ship took off through space so fast that Nigel fell off of his feet.

Once he got up, he said, "That's it, I'm making you pilot."

"Zarsh, get the hell out of that chair. Fred is going to fly this thing."

Tzarcyzk frowned and did as he was told.

"Alright everyone, let's calm down a little," Paul the Viking commanded. "We have some mysteries to destroy. Fred, or Derf, whatever your name is, keep the ship flying at a steady pace."

Paul smiled at how beautiful the stars looked bending all around him. This was truly great. He sat in his luxurious captain's chair. So soft and comfortable, and big like a throne. It was where he belonged.

"Everyone take their seats," he commanded. "Counselor Soo, you stay right there to my left."

Papillon was relieved she didn't have to move and was able to keep doing her nails. She was tripping so hard at this point that fixating on her nails seemed to be the only thing keeping her together. She didn't even really like doing her nails, but she was trying to stay in character really hard and figured a Vietnamese girl would do her nails a lot in her spare time. She thought it was strange there was a whole nail kit on the chair when she walked in, with a file and nail polish and everything, but took it anyway.

Embrace the strange, she thought, and then she quickly looked over her shoulder to see if the white coated rabbit man was hiding behind her. There was no one. She went back to doing her nails.

"Nigel Powerbottom, or Commander Powerbottom, I guess I'll call you, take the seat to my right."

"My name is Nigel *Dickinson*, sir."

"If you say so," Paul snickered.

Nigel sighed, and took his seat.

Next thing you know he'll be making me fetch him tea and crumpets, he thought.

Hmmmm, tea and crumpets though, he pondered. *I sure would fancy a nosh right about now. Blimey, do I really sound that British in my head? It's probably just because these two sound so Scandinavian and... Chinese, probably.*

Nigel probably had figured out that Papillon Soo Soo was not Vietnamese at all, but more likely a Chinese girl. This would prove Nigel Dickinson *is* the smartest man in the room, but there would be ample time for that to come out more so he could perhaps brag about it a bit.

"Derf," Paul said, "You and... what was your name again, kid?"

The alien boy from the future smiled.

"Tzarcyzk-616, sir!"

"Tzarcyzk-616." Paul said, pronouncing it correctly.

SQUEEEEEE! Tzarcyzk thought. *He said my name!*

"You two go take the controls down in the front."

Tzarcyzk was thrilled he still got to be the pilot.

"But we're not going to call Derf Fred, sir?"

"No, man," Paul told him, "I don't think it's that clever that you just spelled his name backwards to create the name Fred. That's just kind of lame."

Fred is his original name spelled backwards?! Nigel thought. *Wow. Mind blown. How humbling.*

"Futuristic Jew Beast," Paul said, addressing Frankenstein.

Frankenstein came forward.

"You stay back there near that console near the door and protect our backs. If anyone comes in we do not know, take care of them for me," Paul asked.

Frankenstein grunted in agreement. If anyone came in he was sure he could sell them something.

"And what about me?" Guy asked.

But he was ignored. So he asked again.

"HEY! What about me?"

It was like he was invisible.

Tzarcyzk-616 turned to Guy and sent a thought message at him. It felt like needles touching the inside of his brain.

"Paul killed you a long time ago, Guy."

"WHAT?!" Guy mindscreamed.

"He murdered you after you challenged him over the captain's chair."

"NO! But that can't be! I'm still here! I'm still real! It's just the acid, I swear!"

"Of course you're still real. You're just a ghost now."

"NOOOO!" Guy screamed.

"Jesus Christ, shut the fuck up, Guy," Paul commanded.

Guy stared at him in shock.

"You... you can hear me?" he asked.

"Of course I can hear you. Everyone can hear you. We're not deaf."

"But I thought you killed me?"

"I *will* kill you if you don't stop flipping out and get to work."

"It's just the acid," Nigel said. "It seems to be affecting us all in different ways."

He leaned in closer to Guy.

"We really thought we lost you there for a second. You were making a right fool of yourself, you were."

"ENOUGH!" Paul shouted, pounding his fist on the arm of his captain's chair.

"Go and fetch us some ale, food, *whatever*, just do your damned job!"

"And what job is that?" Guy asked.

"Ship's chef," Nigel snickered, thrilled someone else was going to be the butler for once. And it was quite fitting that it would be Guy serving a man like Paul. It was what he deserved.

"Oh, goddamn it!" Guy yelled.

He looked at Tzarcyzk, and sneered. Tzarcyzk looked back at him as if nothing had happened. Perhaps it didn't.

Well, if he didn't get to be captain, Guy decided he was going to be one hell of a chef. The crew would have the finest gluten-free and vegan food he could muster, and hopefully he could find something micro-brewed with free range hops and a high alcohol content for them all to drink. Really, it would help take the edge off at this point. He, like everyone else, was really tripping balls. Even Frankenstein, who didn't seem too visibly affected, was still jumping at the sight of his own shadow every now and then. The big guy could probably use a drink as well.

Guy left on the lift to find the galley. He asked the computer where it was and it told him, helping him find it quite easily.

It's nice to not be dead.

"Did anyone else just feel a ghost in here?" Paul asked.

CHAPTER THIRTEEN
CRASH

"Cucumber sandwiches?!"

"Uh, sorry sir, it was the only vegetable I could find in the galley," Guy apologized. "I don't even think the bread is gluten-free."

"Don't apologise, lad. Cucumber sandwiches are my absolute favorite. Smashing!" Nigel said, as Britishly as possible.

Guy offered the plate of sandwiches to Paul, who was already drinking an alien ale he had brought up out of a S.S. Mashrue souvenir glass that Frankenstein had found downstairs.

"Are these gluten free?" Paul asked.

"No, sorry sir, they are not."

Paul lunged at Guy menacingly.

"I'LL KILL YOU!"

Guy covered his face with his hands and cowered before the Viking.

Paul sat back down and laughed.

"HA! Just kidding," he said, grabbing a sandwich. "I don't even know what gluten is. I'm a Viking from the year one-thousand."

Guy had almost pissed himself.

Tzarcyzk-616 had been very busy preparing a lot of note cards in the meantime for the captain to read. He was also sweating profusely, and really heating up quite a bit. He must be feeling the effects of the acid. Without even noticing, he was actually just writing the same message over and over again on all the cards. Except they were all in different languages. From Earth dialects to alien.

Paul belched, and motioned over to Soo Soo.

"Counselor Soo Soo," he commanded. "Status report."

Papillon looked up from what she was doing, slightly annoyed.

"Uh..." she said, trying to remember her lines. "Me love you too much!"

"Very good!" Paul shouted.

And then he asked Nigel too.

"Number One! Status report."

Nigel was confused about whether or not he should say, *"Me love you too much!"* as well, wondering if it would be funny or not. He was just a butler though and not a spaceman, but Paul had been adamant about giving everyone jobs. Then Nigel had an idea.

"ZARSH!" he commanded. He would just relegate the task to another underling. "Status report."

Tzarcyzk-616 rushed up to Nigel and handed him a note card, then he rushed back to his seat.

It just said, *Me love you long time.*

Nigel laughed and put the card face down on his console.

"Well?" Paul asked.

"Oh, it was just rubbish," Nigel said. "Pay it no mind."

"Captain," Derf said, bringing a tablet up to Paul to show him something.

The caveman pointed to the words "S.S. Mashrue" on the tablet.

"Ship." Derf said.

"Yeah," Paul said, "What does that mean, anyway?"

"Star... Smasher?"

"Ha!" Paul said, "What a mighty fine name for a vessel."

Derf pointed to the tablet again, particularly to a bunch of other words on it. Paul tried to make out what they were but couldn't.

"It just looks like a bunch of squiggly lines..." he observed.

And then Tzarcyzk-616 finally mustered the courage to bring his note cards up to Captain Paul. The first one he handed him also had the same squiggly lines on it.

"Is this some kind of language?" Paul asked.

Tzarcyzk nodded.

"But I thought all languages were supposed to be the same now, since we were on LSD. I think the Doctor said so."

Tzarcyzk shook his head, and handed him the next card.

This one was in English. Paul read it out loud.

"S.S. Mashrue is S.S. Enterprise in Arabic. This is an ISIS ship. And when we entered the bridge and turned on the controls we set off a homing beacon. They are going to find us and take their ship back, probably by force."

Paul changed his expression to one of concern.

"That terrorist group? The one we saw in the video?"

Tzarcyzk-616 nodded.

"CAPTAIN!" Nigel screamed.

"WHAT!?" Paul asked, extremely startled.

"We have incoming!"

"On screen!" he shouted.

Derf pressed a button on the controls and the viewscreen changed to show a large, scimitar-shaped vessel approaching their immediate vicinity. It had the squiggly lines written on the outside of the ship too. But under the squiggly lines it also had big letters that plainly spelled out, "S.S. ISIS".

"BY ODIN'S BEARD!" Paul shouted.

"Captain, they're hailing us," Nigel said. "Just like on that show *Star Trek* I was talking about."

Nigel briefly tripped out at the fact that this was exactly *Star Trek*. It was uncanny. This had to be the worst acid trip ever.

"Uh..." Paul said. "Put that on screen too, maybe."

"Derf put," said the caveman pilot, pressing another button.

"AL-KAFIRUN!" a man screamed on the screen.

"BY ODIN'S OTHER BEARD!" Paul shouted, almost jumping out of his chair.

The towel-headed terrorist sneered, looking extra menacing with his creepy robotic eye and beard, like some kind of space pirate.

"AL-KAFIRUN!" he screamed again, and started pressing buttons on his ship's console. They started glowing red.

"What is he doing?!" Paul asked Nigel.

"Whatever it is, it probably isn't good."

"AL-KAFIRUN!" the terrorist screamed again. "TAHTIM KHAZZAM ALFADA ALEIMLAQ!"

Everyone tensed with fear.

"Tzarcyzk-616!" Paul commanded. "Do you know what he is saying?!"

Tzarcyzk started writing down the words and began translating them.

The terrorist pointed at the screen menacingly, and said, "ALLIZAR!"

He made a motion with his finger across his throat as if to cut it. And then he turned off his viewscreen so the crew could just see the view of the S.S. ISIS starship again. The point of the ship at the front end of the scimitar began glowing a brighter and brighter red. It was almost getting to the point where it was blinding.

Paul stared wide-eyed at the screen.

"TZAR?!" he shouted. "WHAT DID HE SAY?!"

Tzarcyzk-616 ran up to the captain with the card. Paul tried to read it, but it looked like he was only able to translate one word.

"What's a lazer?" Paul asked.

Tzarcyzk pointed at the screen.

A gigantic red lazer beam shot out of the ISIS

ship and hit the Star Smasher with devastating force. The shockwave coursed through the ship, knocking out all systems and causing fires everywhere. The crew were violently tossed around the bridge as the lazer blast exploded around them.

When the ship stopped shaking, Paul picked himself up and got back in his captain's chair.

"Well, that was the worst thing ever."

He looked around at his crew.

"Is everyone all right?"

Frankenstein said, "*RAAAAA!*" He held Papillon Soo Soo in his arms. She seemed to have been knocked unconscious and was bleeding profusely from her head.

"FRANKENSTEIN!" Nigel shouted, "TAKE HER TO THE MEDICAL BAY IMMEDIATELY!"

Frankenstein turned around only to find flames on the wall, and freaked out, screamed, dropped Soo Soo, and waved his arms around in the air, yelling, "FIRE BAD!"

He had dropped Soo Soo on her head.

"HELP HER, NUMBER ONE!" Paul shouted.

"GODDAMNIT, MAN!" Nigel screamed. "I'M NOT A DOCTOR!"

Guy stepped in, taking advantage of the opportunity.

"*I'll* be the doctor," he told the captain. "I took a CPR class at the community center, so I'm sure I can save her."

"Fine!" Paul said. "Just get her away from

Frankenstein over there before he stomps her to death!"

Guy went and grabbed her and slung her over his shoulder as Tzarcyzk-616 put out the fires on the wall and computer consoles with a pen-sized fire extinguisher. It shot out a tiny white cloud and looked trippy as hell.

Paul became fixated on it for a second before he snapped out of it and yelled, "TZARCYZK-616! DAMAGE REPORT!"

Tzarcyzk ran up to the captain and handed him another note card.

It said, *The shields absorbed the brunt of the impact.*

Paul looked up at him. "Is that good?"

Tzarcyzk wrote another note card.

Yes, it said. *But it also knocked out the ship's power, and without it, the ship cannot fully function at the capacity that it needs to.*

"And what does that mean, exactly?"

Tzarcyzk started writing out another card.

Paul smacked the pen out of his hand.

"CUT THAT OUT! JUST TELL ME WHAT IT MEANS!"

Tzarcyzk looked up at the captain nervously.

"It means we're going to crash."

"ALL HANDS BRACE FOR IMPACT!" Paul shouted.

Nigel put his seat belt on, wondering how Paul always knew all these space captain-like things to say. It must be the LSD, he figured.

Derf brought something up on the screen and

pointed at it to show the captain. It was a green-colored planet.

"Ship go," Derf said as he pointed to the planet.

"OK CREW! WE'RE GOING DOWN!" Paul said.

Tzarcyzk-616 helped strap Frankenstein into a chair, and ran back over to his console and got on the controls, working with Derf to try to pull the ship up so it didn't crash head first into the ground. If they could clear a few trees it might help soften the impact.

Nigel saw a man in a white laboratory coat out of the corner of his eye. He appeared to be fumbling with the controls. But when he looked in that direction he had disappeared...

And the Star Smasher crashed into the planet below.

CHAPTER FOURTEEN
THE GREEN PLANET

Everyone was dead. Paul sat eviscerated in his captain's chair. His guts stretched from his seat to the elevator shaft, where Guy had apparently tripped over them and fell to his death. Tzarcyzk-616's face had smashed into his control console upon impact, and was completely obliterated. Derf was stuck in the wall across the room, broken bones jutting out of his carcass, all death-like. Nigel was sitting in his chair with his legs crossed, smiling. His brains were slowly leaking out the back of his head. Frankenstein was never technically alive anyway, but he was picking over the crew, checking their pockets for money and stealing their wrist watches.

Papillon Soo Soo was sitting against the wall, still unconscious and bleeding from the head. But she woke up, and slowly opened her eyes to see the carnage. And then she noticed the elusive man in the white labcoat in the corner. He noticed her too, and started creeping towards her, hands stretched out before him like he was going to get her.

"Doctor Yes?" she asked. "Is this the future?"

And then he reached out and grabbed her.

She closed her eyes and screamed in terror.

"PAPILLON!" Guy shook her.

She opened her eyes. It was just that douchebag hipster, Guy. The whole thing must've been a dream.

"ARE. YOU. OK?" Guy asked, pausing between each word to make sure she could understand.

Papillon tried to slip back into character.

"Hey you Guy..." she said in her Vietnamese accent. "Me have Swedish headache," she said, holding her temples and moaning. "Me love you long time, baby."

"A headache?" Guy asked, which was kind of all he could understand. "I have just the thing for that!"

He pulled a roll of seaweed out of the sushi box he found in the galley and started wrapping it around her head.

"That should keep all the blood in," Guy said, proud of himself for being the best doctor ever.

"Now come on, let's get back to the bridge. I have to see if everyone else is OK."

He grabbed the seaweed, soy sauce, and wasabi, as if packing supplies for a first aid kit.

Back on the bridge, everyone was pretty much OK. The seat belts really worked. Guy noticed that Nigel had a small paper cut on his finger though and tried to rub wasabi in it.

"SOD OFF!" Nigel screamed, slapping Guy's hands away. "Now go get us all some tea!" He dismissed Guy.

Papillon took her seat back next to the captain, who noticed her head was wrapped in seaweed, but figured it must be an Asian thing since she seemed to be better.

"STATUS REPORT!" Paul shouted.

Papillon screamed.

"Oh, sorry Counselor Soo," Paul said. "I didn't mean to startle you."

She gave him a dirty look. She was almost done saying things in character. And she could feel that the effects of the LSD were wearing off completely.

Everyone else must be feeling it too, she wondered. *And maybe that's a good thing.*

Paul cleared his throat, and yelled again to no one in general, "DAMAGE REPORT!"

Nigel was blowing on his hot cup of tea that Guy had brought him. He looked towards the captain.

"Well, which is it, mate? Damage report or status report?"

Paul slammed down another alien ale (his fifth since they were attacked by ISIS), wiped the foam from his mouth, and belched.

He just stared into space. Or the wall where space used to be. On the viewscreen. Which was now just cracked and broken, with some gray smoke coming out of it.

"Uh..." Paul said, trying to find his thoughts.

"Give me a, uh, *status report* on the *damage report*."

"In a minute," Nigel said. "I don't want my tea to get cold."

Paul looked at Papillon, who was doing her nails again.

"Counselor Soo?" he asked.

Without looking up at him, she just said, "Anytin you want, baby."

Paul waited.

"Well?" he asked her again.

No answer.

Paul sighed.

"Where the fuck is that smart kid, the one with the note cards?" Paul asked.

A note card appeared in front of Paul's face that said, *Right behind you.*

Paul screamed.

Tzarcyzk-616 was standing right behind Paul, as if he had been waiting to help him.

"Well?" Paul asked. "Give me the details."

Tzarcyzk cleared his throat and went to the front of the room where he pulled out the note cards he had written. With the newfound confidence the captain gave him, he started to read them out loud.

"We have crashed on an uncharted class-5 planet which, according to the ship's computer, has not been conquered by ISIS, even though they occupy most of this system."

"TERRORIST FIENDS!" Paul yelled.

He then got up to make a speech, brandishing his fist dramatically.

"They will pay for what they've done to my ship! Start repairs! In the meantime, we will conquer this planet in the name of our people! In the name of Earth! We shall pillage the land! Take all of its resources! Take all of its women! And ISIS will rue the day they ever crossed us!"

He sat down and opened another ale, and started

chugging it so hard most just spilled out the sides of his mouth and soaked his big red beard.

Derf walked up to Tzarcyzk with his computer tablet, and pointed to certain points that needed fixing on the map of the ship displayed on the screen.

"Ship fix," Derf said.

Tzarcyzk relayed this to the captain.

"Engineer Derf says the ship is broken really bad in several places and it will take two days to repair."

"Very good!" Paul said. "Derf, get on that immediately."

Paul stood up and addressed the crew.

"That gives us two days to explore and conquer this new planet, gather supplies, meet the local people, fuck them, maybe kill them, and relax."

That seemed to be OK with everybody.

"We will split up into three teams of two," Paul said.

"First team—Tzarcyzk and Guy. I want you two to gather food and intel on this world. If you find any of its women, bring me all of its women. Tzarcyzk, takes notes on everything you see. I want a full report when we meet up again."

Tzarcyzk nodded.

"HEY!" Guy said, "Why do I have to be stuck with the weirdo?"

Tzarcyzk frowned a little. He was looking forward to having a bit of alone time with Guy so they could discuss Free Greenpeace.

But now it just sounded like Guy was going to be a dick the whole time.

"Do as you're told! Or I will smite you!" Paul threatened.

"Next team—Nigel and Counselor Soo, I want you two to, uh..." Paul tried to think.

"Uh... do the exact thing Tzarcyzk and Guy will be doing, I guess."

Some leadership, Papillon thought.

"Uh, and Captain?" Nigel asked, raising his hand.

"Yes, Number One?"

"If you're a captain, and I'm a commander, shouldn't everyone else get their correct designations too? And what about last names? I should be addressed as Commander Dickinson all the time, not Nigel. And you haven't even told us your last name."

Paul pondered this for a second, and said, "NAH! We don't need to go by any last names. I mean, hey—look at Frankenstein," he pointed over to Frankenstein, and everyone looked at him.

"Frankenstein only has one name, and he's pretty good."

The green monster grumbled.

My name's not even really Frankenstein, he thought.

Paul was actually just deflecting the question, because he didn't want Nigel to know that they shared the same last name—Dickinson. Hell, they look like they could actually even be a little related. If Paul got a haircut and shaved, there might even be a slight resemblance. And Paul didn't like that, since he considered Nigel to be a bit of a dandy and not a real man like himself.

"Anyway," Paul continued, "you can all just address me as *Captain*. Although I don't mind you calling me by my first name when needed. Just let's not make a habit out of it, OK? Soo Soo is Counselor Soo, like we already established. And everyone make sure to address Nigel as Commander Dickinson. He *is* second-in-command and you will all treat him with the same respect you do me, your captain leader."

Paul pondered something for a second, "And actually, let's *all* treat each other with respect. Because that is a great way to be a good team."

Paul looked over to Guy and pointed to him.

"Except for that Guy, he's a dick."

"HEY!" Guy yelled, and then crossed his arms in a huff.

"And Nigel, I'd still like to call you Number One, if that's alright."

"Jolly good, Captain," Nigel smiled.

"And Derf and Tzarcyzk-616 will be," he turned to Nigel again, "What was that, Number One? Lieutenants?"

Commander Dickinson nodded.

"Yes, Captain."

"And what was that name you wanted Derf to have? Fred?"

"Yes, Captain," Nigel smiled. "Just like Fred Flintstone. It was a caveman cartoon show on the telly when I was a lad. *Quite* entertaining."

"OK then. So, Lieutenant Fred, and Lieutenant Tzarcyzk, which I think we'll also address with that shortened name you gave him, Zarsh. So, Lieutenant Zarsh."

Tzarcyzk-616 frowned. He did not think his name was that hard to pronounce. In the future where he came from, everyone had names like his. And it was pronounced exactly how it was spelled. "Suh-zar-zick-six-sixteen". Not so hard. But nonetheless, Tzarcyzk was happy that he was lieutenant, and was pretty sure no one was going to stick to the right names and designations anyway. Especially the captain, who seemed to be getting drunk as fuck.

"And Frankenstein and Guy... let's see..."

"Well, obviously, it's *Doctor* Guy now, Captain," Guy boasted, pointing to Papillon Soo Soo's head, that he had wrapped up in seaweed to stop the bleeding.

"More like *Gay* Guy," Nigel snickered.

Paul started laughing his ass off.

"HA! That's it then! Guy will be Gay Guy from now on!"

Guy frowned.

"HEY!" he said in disagreement.

Paul continued laughing.

"And Frankenstein, you get to be *Doctor* Frankenstein."

"HEY!" Guy shouted again, in a classically Gay Guy way.

Frankenstein grunted. Dr. Frankenstein was his creator. And he was a very bad man. Frankenstein didn't like this one bit. So he decided to speak up about it.

"DOCTOR FRANKENSTEIN BAD!"

"That's right, Doctor Frankenstein! You *are* bad. *Bad ass!*" Paul said.

"*RAAAA!*" Frankenstein roared, so loud it shook Paul's alien ale glass.

"And that's why I want you on my team, you're the strongest here and I want the best warrior at my side. This planet is sure to not be tame, but with us two together, nothing can stand in our way," Paul said, in his thick Scandinavian accent, which he'd been talking in the whole time.

"Frankenstein!" Frankenstein shouted, as if to agree with Paul on the team-up.

"OK then," Paul clapped his hands together. "Let's go see what weapons they have in the armory and then we'll be on our way."

Everyone followed the leader onto the lift and down to a part of the ship they hadn't been to yet, which was probably near the exit doors to the outside.

The elevator worked because the caveman had presumably already fixed the power a little.

Hell, he could have fixed half the ship already while the captain was talking, you don't even know.

CHAPTER FIFTEEN
THE ARMORY

As the effects of the LSD had obviously completely worn off by now, and everyone seemed to be alright and feeling fine, even though this was supposed to be more of a fish-out-of-water story about time displaced people being thrown together in the future, and a French-Chinese actress was still pretending to be a Vietnamese prostitute for some reason while her head was wrapped in seaweed—the armory was full of really cool futuristic lazer weapons.

There were lazer rifles, lazer pistols, lazer swords, armored knee pads, armored elbow pads, armored chest pieces, and really cool helmets that said "Lazer Tag" on the side, where the word "Lazer" was clearly spelled with a *Z*, and not an *S*.

No one grabbed any of the padded armor. The captain, Paul the Viking from 11th Century Norway, grabbed the lazer sword, Counselor Soo picked up a gigantic lazer rifle and slung it over her back with the strap, Lieutenant Zarsh picked up a couple of lazer pistols, Commander Dickinson took two lazer pistols, two lazer rifles, and a lazer sword as he was pretty much scared to death to go outside on the alien planet, and

Guy and Frankenstein didn't pick up anything.

"Guess you don't need a weapon, huh, Dr. Frankenstein?" Paul asked, again—in his thick Norwegian accent that he obviously has and always talks in.

Frankenstein shook his head.

"Of course not," Paul said. "Because you *are* the weapon."

Frankenstein nodded his head.

"And how about you, Gay Guy? If anyone needs a weapon, it would be you."

Guy scoffed.

"I'm against guns, of any kind. They should be banned. I will not take part in any kind of violence. I bet you anything, one of you will accidentally shoot someone and you'll see that when you play with fire, you get burned."

"FIRE!?" Frankenstein yelled. "FIRE BAD!"

"Calm down, Dr. Frankenstein. There is no fire, Gay Guy is just being a pacifist little bitch," Paul reassured the giant green monster.

"FRANKENSTEIN GOOD," the monster responded.

Nigel dumped out a box of devices he found on to the table.

"Everyone, look, there's a bunch of things in here we might find useful."

"Communication devices!" Lieutenant Zarsh noted.

"Yes, we should all grab one of these so we can stay in contact whenever we need to."

Nigel picked one up. It was a big silver letter *Z*.

"I think they would go nicely right on the breast of our uniforms, pinned on."

He showed everyone how to do it, and then pressed it to turn it on, giving an example of how to use it to communicate. It was exactly like that show *Star Trek: The Next Generation*, even though Nigel had never seen it. Because it had never existed.

Nigel also sorted through the rest of the tech on the table and grabbed some cool stuff like little hand-held scanners and things of that sort, which looked like nifty scientific instruments. Papillon and Guy grabbed some too. The three of them were obviously more tech-interested, being from the last three decades and all. Paul wondered why the threesome were basically from the same era and no one else from his era was chosen for the... *is this an experiment or something?*

He wondered but honestly couldn't remember why they were all there in the first place. But he shrugged off the thought, and focused on the task at hand. He was very excited to take their new lazer weapons onto the new planet and explore it. It was something beyond his wildest dreams as a Viking. And he was definitely going to make the most of it.

He grabbed two cases of alien ale and made Frankenstein hold them.

"You look strong enough to carry these the whole time," Paul told him. "If we get attacked by some kind of aliens or something, let me take care of them. Protect the beer. If I need help, put the cases down gently and help me fight. Try not to break any of the bottles."

Frankenstein nodded.

"OK crew," Paul said all captainly, about to command to the crew. "Let's roll out!"

Papillon pressed a button to open the exit doors, and they opened to display the wonders of a whole new alien world.

"*OOOOOH,*" the whole team marveled at once.

CHAPTER SIXTEEN
EXPEDITION

The planet was a lush green jungle full of life and beauty. It was pretty much like earth, except totally alien, complete with talking pineapples (probably). Big patches of the ground appeared to be shag carpet from the '70s. Monkey-lizard-birds were part of the local ecosystem and not just hallucinations. It also had more details about it that would make it seem more like Earth than an alien planet, but those are boring details and who wants to bore you here? Certainly not the author. Look, there are probably giant snakes you can ride complete with saddles and everything, so who cares that there are babbling creeks, a Starbucks, and clear, blue skies?

The terrain was lush and vibrant, yet there were trails cut through the thick bracken. And as the presence of giant saddle snakes was just a mere probability, the crew would set out on foot. At first the team did not know where to go, but it was just generally decided to split off into three different directions. That way the teams would cover more ground, Paul figured.

The planet was so alien, and big and weird, that the team was actually happy to not be tripping balls anymore. It was such an amazing sight anyway that it was just great to be enjoying it naturally with a clear mind. Papillon even thought for sure she was going to stop acting like a Vietnamese prostitute soon. *Soon.*

She was just waiting for the right moment. She and her teammate, Commander Dickinson, had stopped at the end of a path at a gigantic, beautiful waterfall. He pointed one of his handheld science scanners at it like he was taking readings.

"Nigel?" she asked. "I have something to tell you."

Nigel didn't even look up from his scanner.

"Let me guess," he said. "You're not actually a Vietnamese prostitute."

Then he looked at her to gauge her reaction.

She looked like a deer caught in the headlights.

"What?" she gasped. "How did you..."

"I've seen Full Metal Jacket, you know. You were quite wonderful in it."

"I'm still going to be in it?" she asked.

"Of course! It even says so right here on your IMDB page."

Nigel showed her the screen on his science scanner. He was actually just looking at the internet the whole time. A handheld device that had it readily accessible was still new to him, but he was well familiar with the internet in his era and especially the Internet Movie Database, his favorite movie site. He was quite the film buff.

Papillon was a little shocked to see it.

"And the film, it did good?"

Nigel smiled at her.

"Of course. It was critically acclaimed. It even won a few Academy Awards, if I remember correctly."

"Oh my..." Papillon beamed.

Nigel smiled at her again.

"Nice accent, by the way. Good to meet a fellow Brit out here in the far reaches of space."

"Oh, Nigel," she took his hand. "I agree."

Nigel leaned in and she kissed him passionately in a warm embrace.

"Sucky-sucky?" Nigel joked.

Papillon laughed.

"Oh Nigel, me love you long time."

They both had a good laugh and continued kissing, and ended up flat on the ground where they made sweet British love.

Meanwhile, somewhere else, Captain Paul the Viking was doing something too. He and Frankenstein had stopped so they could have an alien ale. It was very hot and humid on this planet, which was something neither of them was used to. Frankenstein had spent all winter in a concentration camp, and Paul was from Norway, and had spent all winter in Norway, where it was cold.

Captain Paul the Viking grabbed another alien ale out of the case, cracked it open and took a big swig. Frankenstein took two bottles and bit the tops off with his teeth, then chewed and swallowed the glass. Paul looked at him in amazement.

"Woah!" he said. "Monster man, that was totally brutal."

He raised his beer, and said cheers in his native tongue.

"SKÅL!"

Frankenstein held up his beers and said, "PROST!"

Paul wondered why he had said *prost* instead of *skål*, forgetting that Frankenstein is German.

It is probably just the LSD, he thought. *That is the reason to describe everything that is wrong.*

Paul swigged his beer, made a thirst-quenched sound, got up and stretched.

That's when he noticed a village down the hill.

"*Oooh!*" Paul got all excited. "Frankenstein! Look! There's a village down the hill!"

Frankenstein went over and looked with him.

"*Rargh!*" he said.

"And look! It's full of green-skinned people! Just like you!"

"Rargh!" Frankenstein grumbled.

"Do you want to go down there and rape and pillage them with me?"

"RARGH!"

Paul took that as a *yes*.

"Come then, green monster. I will ignite my lazer sword and we will kill their men and fuck their women and steal their shit."

Then Paul lost his footing, drunkenly, and slid down the hill face first to the outskirts of the village.

"RAAAAA!" Frankenstein screamed, concerned.

Paul rubbed the dirt out of his eyes and got up and looked at the alien creatures around him.

They all had spears pointed at him. They were green-scaled, lizard-like people with solid black eyes, flesh mohawks, and long, whipping tails.

Paul stood up and brandished his lazer sword. He pressed the button on the handle but nothing came out. But he still made lazer sounds with his mouth, like "WHIRROW! ZZZZUH! CRAASH!" and waved it around like it was deadly.

The lizard men jumped back a little. But when they saw there was no danger, they pressed on again with the sharp end of their sticks pointed at Paul.

One shouted something at him in a crazy alien language.

Paul put his hands up.

"Look, man. I don't speak terrorist, OK?"

The lizard man just looked at him, and then Paul lunged forward with his lazer sword, and this time it worked.

A white hot beam of light sizzled and zapped out of the handle, freaking the shit out of the aliens, who were all clearly startled. They lowered their weapons in awe. Unfortunately, it also freaked out Paul a little. It was so blindingly bright that he couldn't see, and the handle got so hot that it started burning his hand and he had to drop it.

"OW!" he screamed, shaking his hand in pain.

Paul rubbed his eyes, and when his vision refocused a little, he saw all the green alien men running away in terror.

"HA!" he shouted.

And then he felt a tap on his shoulder.

It was Frankenstein behind him. He had finally made his way down and the mere sight of him must've scared off the alien creatures.

"Frankenstein! Raaa!" Frankenstein said.

"Well, thanks. I guess." Paul said, a little upset that it was Frankenstein who scared off the creatures, and not him.

Then a bunch of flaming arrows began flying at them and Frankenstein started screaming.

"FIRE BAD!"

Paul ducked.

"Come on, Frankenstein. Let's withdraw into the tree cover!"

But it was too late; they were suddenly surrounded by lizard people pointing bows with flaming arrows at them, while some of them held torches.

The fire glared upon them.

"FIRE BAD!" Frankenstein screamed, shielding his face with his arms.

Paul put his hands up, and said, "Don't worry Frankenstein, I'll get us out of this."

The lizard men threw nets onto Paul and Frankenstein and dragged them away. They were put into a big wooden cage in the center of town, surrounded by green people and fire, like they were trapped in some kind of *green inferno*. Paul figured that they were probably going to cut them up and eat them, but he had a plan.

He tapped on his communicator pin. He heard it make a *blip* sound and assumed it was working.

"Crew," he said. "This is your captain speaking. Frankenstein and I have been captured by lizard people. I am sure that they are going to try to eat us. Please follow the coordinates on my, uh... *tracking device* or something, and save us. Come close to their village and shoot your lazer pistols at them until they have all met death."

Frankenstein growled to get Paul's attention.

"BEER!" Frankenstein reminded him.

"Oh!" Paul said, tapping on his communicator pin again. "We left the beer at the top of the hill. Be sure to bring it."

Frankenstein smiled.

Paul smiled too. Sometimes things were so easy to get out of when you had someone else do all the work for you.

Somewhere far away, Tzarcyzk and Guy were off on their own adventure, and actually getting more done than anyone.

Guy had foraged for a lot of vegan foods, like greens and berries. Apparently alien planets had the same kind of food as Earth, so it was all good. Hell, Tzarcyzk-616 is from another planet as well, and *he* thought it was all good.

They also found a lot of sparkly crystals, shiny arrowheads, and souvenir-sized gold pyramids. They definitely reminded Tzarcyzk of something, so he decided now was the right time to tell Guy about it.

He started to write it all down on a note card first. He told Guy he had to go to the bathroom, but that really was just a lie because he needed some alone time to prepare his notes and practice what he was going to say. He had to put it delicately and still get his point across, yet be captivating enough that Guy would want to pay attention.

Guy went back to foraging for alien-variety vegan food and Tzarcyzk-616 found a nice clearing behind some bushes to be alone.

"Hey Guy, it's me, that guy from the future who called you," Tzarcyzk read off of his card, totally trying to do a normal guy voice. "I am a normal guy just like you and I talk like *this*."

Tzarcyzk thought he just sounded like he was trying too hard to do an American accent. He sighed and crumpled up the note card and threw it away.

What was he doing wrong? He decided maybe he should talk more like the captain, who seemed to be able to talk right all time, and always said the right things he meant to say. Tzarcyzk-616 looked at Paul the Viking as a pillar of strength, and a source of mirth and inspiration.

He read the next card like Paul, trying to pull off a Norwegian accent.

"Hey Guy, you are like small girl. You need help, so I travel from future. You see, I am awesome and tall, and yet so handsome. You need big strong man like me to save the day."

Sigh, Tzarcyzk thought, thinking the word like it's spelled. *I sound too Russian.*

He crumpled up the card, and then sighed for real.

Then he heard a terrible scream!

Tzarcyzk-616 dropped all of his cards and ran to go see what was amiss.

A gigantic tentacle had Guy in its grip and pulled him away deep into the jungle.

"TZARCYZK! HELP ME!" Guy screamed.

"OK!"

Tzarcyzk ran inhumanly fast and caught up to the gigantic tentacle in no time, and jumped right on to a big bulgy part of it and started frantically shooting the thing with both lazer pistols.

Really cool lazer blast sounds shot out of them, along with the deadly hot lazer beams they're designed to shoot out since they're weapons and not toys. The tentacle relinquished its grip as an animalistic scream roared in the distance.

Tzarcyzk jumped through the air and caught Guy before he fell to the ground, where they both landed safely.

"Jesus christ, dude! Are you The Six Million Dollar Man?!"

Tzarcyzk didn't get the reference, and just gave Guy a puzzled look.

"Sorry, you probably don't get the reference. Hell, sometimes I forget you're from the future. From a whole different world! Six million dollars is probably nothing where you come from. You're probably more of a... six *trillion* dollar man."

Tzarcyzk shook his head. He still didn't understand the reference.

"A ROBOT!" Guy screamed.

Tzarcyzk nodded. All of the people of his homeworld were robots. Hell, most people from the future were robots too. It was a very robotic future. That was just normal.

"Well, cool, I always wanted to be friends with a robot," Guy said. "The people in Portland suck so much. I don't even really get along with any of them. I would get a dog, but I'm allergic to them. Dogs are much better than people. But a robot is *way* better than a dog. If I had it my way, Portland would just be nothing but robots. I bet *that* would save the environment. I bet robots are pretty green."

"Guy," Tzarcyzk-616 put his hands on his shoulders. "Listen to me."

Tzarcyzk-616 looked Guy straight in the eyes.

"It's that kind of thinking that's going to destroy your future."

Guy looked a little shocked, but he maintained eye contact. He believed every word Tzarcyzk said.

"I came back in time to help you. I found your Free Greenpeace flyer at a museum of Earth's history. I was the one who talked to you on the phone. But I arrived in your city ten years too late, and all of it was destroyed. It was a land of ashes. A devastating force had taken over. A great pyramid with a giant eye fixed its gaze upon me and sent a legion of deadly lazer robots to kill me. It was the most apocalyptic thing I've ever seen, and I've rented almost every Earth disaster movie from the museum's library."

"The pyramid... the eye..." Guy pondered. "The Illuminati?!"

"No," Tzarcyzk said, shooting down the theory. "I don't think it had anything to do with ancient conspiracy theories."

Tzarcyzk reached into his pocket and pulled out one of the golden pyramid souvenirs.

"I think it has everything to do with *this*."

"An alien pyramid?" Guy asked.

"Yes. I think it is the same race of beings that ISIS must be fighting out here in the far corners of space. I think they haven't conquered this planet because this is where they're from. And also, I think I know why these aliens are on your Earth."

"Why?" Guy asked.

"Because ISIS was defeated by a combined alliance of the United States, Russia, and France in 2023. Without ISIS to stop them, the ancient aliens took over the planet in just three years. It was one of the reasons ISIS formed, because they knew of a prophecy that would destroy the Earth, and in the future, the remnants of their military, designed time travel technology to go back throughout time to assassinate alien culprits."

"Like that attack on the set of that TV show in the 60s?"

"Yes, exactly like that. One of the cast members was actually an alien. His name was James Doohan. Most of these aliens have a moustache to cover up their true appearance."

"What, like a harelip??"

"Yes, but only more horrifying. That's where an extra mouth on their face can open up. Inside, is a stalk with a third eye, and the eye shoots lazers."

"NO WAY!" Guy said, now thinking that everyone he's ever met with a moustache was actually an alien who shot lazers out of their mouth.

"And anyway, these aliens must be nearby. We should either try to do whatever we can to stop them, or get the hell out of here as fast as we can."

"I guess we should ask the captain," Guy said.

"Good idea," Tzarcyzk pressed his communicator pin to try to hail the captain, as the pair started walking towards his last known location.

"Your dialogue is getting really good, by the way."

"Thank you, Guy."

Tzarcyzk smiled. It was nice to be able to finally talk right.

CHAPTER SEVENTEEN
PAPILLON AND NIGEL: A LOVE STORY

No story is complete without a romance. No tale should be told where a main character is without a love interest. Every book should have a sex scene. And it should usually be between a man and a woman, not two dudes.

Papillon and Nigel cuddled Britishly...

They were both naked.

"So," Nigel asked, holding Papillon in his arms. "How was it?"

"Oh, Nigel, it was fantastic," she said, petting his sexy chest hair.

"And everything was OK... in the *downstairs* area?"

Nigel alluded to his small penis.

"Of course! I loved it."

"It's not... too small?"

Papillon laughed.

"Nigel, we're from England, your penis is the same size as every other man I've ever slept with. Hell, it's probably even a little bigger than most."

Nigel smiled. He couldn't believe it. He actually had a bigger penis than most Brits. This was amazing!

Papillon got up and stretched.

"YAWN!" she said. "I'm a bit hungry. I sure could go for a nosh."

"Well," Nigel said, admiring the view of her naked body, "the captain did say to look for food."

"Hmmm, I think I spot something over there near those trees."

"Well, let's go look," Nigel said, and he took her hand and they went and explored.

"Mushrooms," Papillon leaned down and observed. "*Mmmmm...*"

"Papillon, don't! Those might be poisonous!"

She picked up a handful and ate them anyway.

"Mmmmm! Nigel, you've got to try these, they're SO GOOD!"

"I sincerely doubt alien mushrooms are going to be any..."

She had shoved one in his mouth while he was talking. He chewed it up a little.

"...*good*." His mind changed quickly. "Those are SO GOOD!"

"Let's eat more!"

And Papillon and Nigel ate the mushrooms, moaning in ecstasy, their naked bodies moist with pleasure.

Then Papillon saw the man in the white lab coat again from far away, and gasped.

"Nigel, look! It's the magic man! He's come to get us!"

Nigel looked and saw the man she was talking about. He looked like a big white rabbit from here. And it noticed them, and turned and ran away.

Nigel giggled.

"I bet we can catch him!"

He grabbed her by the hand and off they ran naked into the jungle, after a man who may or may not have been there.

But the jungle came to life, and whispered...

"He's there!" *"And over there."* *"No, he's over here!"* from every which direction.

"Blimey!" Nigel said. "The trees are talking to us."

Then the sky turned red and started dripping colors. Yellow and blue, and what looked like new colors, dripped all around them.

"Oooooh!" Papillon moaned in wonder. "It's so beautiful!"

Then a big shiny rocket ship landed in the clearing. Looking small at first, then bigger and bigger, it landed and made a cloud like a mushroom.

A door opened, and a man walked out dressed like an Egyptian god.

"SUN RA!" Nigel exclaimed. "I'm such a big fan!"

Nigel and Papillon ran up excitedly to meet him.

"Hello, Earthlings. I am Sun Ra. I come from another planet to this planet to bring you back to my planet. And that planet is in space. That's the place."

"Ooooh, I want to go to there!" Papillon said.

"It is a better place to be," Sun Ra offered.

"Better than the Earth?" Nigel asked.

"Planet Earth can't even be sufficient without the rain. It doesn't produce rain, you know. Sunshine... it doesn't produce the sun. The wind... it doesn't produce the wind. All planet Earth produces is... the dead bodies of humanity. That's its only creation. Everything else comes from outer space... from unknown regions. Humanity's life depends on the unknown. Knowledge is... laughable when attributed to a human being."

"WOW!" Nigel said.

"TEACH US, SUN RA, TEACH US!" Papillon commanded.

Sun Ra reached out his hands, and each of them took one and went with him onto his spaceship, which rocketed them off into the sky and far away.

Then Papillon and Nigel woke up in a bamboo cage with Paul and Frankenstein, still naked—not in a rocket with the space man.

"Captain Paul?" Papillon asked. "What happened?"

"You two have been rolling around giggling ever since the lizard men threw you in here."

Nigel gasped, and covered up his penis with his hands immediately, what little there was of it.

"Yes, Number One. I saw your small penis," Paul said, rolling his eyes.

Nigel had never been so embarrassed. Having another guy see his penis was almost worse than a girl seeing it sometimes. He actually had grown to respect Paul a lot and worried his small penis would negatively affect their relationship.

"Is it OK?" Nigel asked.

"Sure, I've seen smaller, I guess."

Paul had actually had sex with some British men before on a conquest. Sometimes he preferred men over there because a lot of the women were so horribly ugly, and at least being with men was different.

"In a gay way?" Nigel asked.

"You bet," Paul winked at him.

This was getting way too gay for Nigel. He was uncomfortable with it. He changed the subject.

"So what are we going to do, Captain?"

"Oh," Paul said. "I didn't mean I was actually interested. Sorry."

Nigel got red faced immediately with embarrassment.

"*No!*" Nigel quickly protested. "That's not what I meant. I meant, what are we going to do about being captured?"

"Oh, that," Paul said. "Don't worry about that. I've called for help on the communicator. I figure Tzarcyzk and Guy will be here shortly, and then they'll shoot all the lizard men with their lazers, and bring us pints of beer."

"FRANKENSTEIN HUNGRY!" the monster roared.

"Oh yeah," Paul remembered. "We're pretty hungry. You guys got anything to eat?"

Even though they were thrown naked in a cage, Papillon and Nigel were surprised to see what they had clenched in their hands. They couldn't believe they didn't notice until now. They opened their hands and revealed big handfuls of the mushrooms that they must have picked from the field.

"Just these alien mushrooms," Papillon said.

"Yeah, you've got to try these, Captain," Nigel offered. "They're pretty amazing."

"Well, give them here." Paul took a handful and started chowing down on them. So did Frankenstein.

Paul looked puzzled for a second and asked, "Hey Counselor Soo, when did you start talking like Nigel?"

"I'm British," she said.

"I thought you were from Vietnam."

"I can still talk like that if you want," she giggled.

"Oh, please do. I love when you do."

"Alright," Papillon said, and slipped back into her Vietnamese accent. "Anytin you want. Me so horny! Me love you long time!"

"HAHAHAHA!" Paul laughed. "It doesn't even make any sense. I love it!"

Papillon smiled. She wondered what it will be like to win an Oscar someday.

Then suddenly, a big shiny flying pyramid floated overhead, causing such a wind that the bamboo cage flew off of the group. Lightning struck all around. A big eye shone red from the peak and started shooting gigantic red lazers in every direction.

"HOLY SHIT!" Paul shouted. "IS THIS EVEN HAPPENING?!"

"Probably not," Nigel replied. "We saw some totally mental shit earlier that likely wasn't there."

"Yeah," Papillon confirmed. "A big black man with a spaceship. It was pretty cool."

"Don't worry, it's just these alien mushrooms. They're a million times better than the LSD the

Doctor gave us on the Star Smasher. Kick back and enjoy the show."

"Oh, OK," Paul said.

They all laid back on the grass and looked at the sky, watching as the alien spaceship shot lazers everywhere. The lizard men screamed and burned all around them as their village was razed.

The group ate mushrooms.

When Guy and Tzarcyzk finally made it to them, they were *all* naked and engaged in psychedelic group sex. Papillon had Frankenstein's enormous green cock in her mouth, Nigel was on the ground eating out her pussy, and below him, Paul was sucking his tiny tallywacker while masturbating.

Tzarcyzk dropped the cases of beer in shock, and the glass bottles shattered. He couldn't believe his eyes.

"Ha-ha! Fags!" Guy taunted as he pointed at them.

Papillon took Frankenstein's big green dick out of her mouth and took a deep breath.

"You guys care to join us?"

"What?!" Guy said, caught a little off guard.

"Oh, I mean... *you want sucky-sucky? Me love you long time!*"

Paul took Nigel's dick out of his mouth.

"No, not him," he said, looking at Guy. "The boy though? Sure."

Tzarcyzk blushed.

"Gay Guy can watch though."

"HEY!" Guy said, pissed off that he was being

called gay by someone who just had a dick in his mouth.

"Oh Captain, keep doing it that way," Nigel said. "You're going to make me cum."

"Then not yet," Paul said. "I'm going to have to fuck you in the ass first, and show you what it's like. And then, and *only then,* do you have my permission to cum."

"Yes, Daddy!"

Nigel bent over for Paul, and Paul spit in his hand and rubbed it all over his thick, big cock, and slid it up Nigel's soft ass.

"OH MY GOD!" he screamed. "FUCK ME!"

"Tzarcyzk!" Papillon shouted. "You get over here and fuck me too! Me so horny!"

Tzarcyzk complied, saying, "Well, I *am* fully functional."

He smiled and took off his clothes and slid his erect future-boy cock into Papillon's wet vagina. Frankenstein sat down and started jerking off while he watched everyone.

Guy sat from far away and watched; actually miffed he didn't get to join in. He wouldn't have minded experimenting a bit, if he had been invited. He couldn't believe Paul was such a dick to him all the time. He wished he could get revenge somehow. Hell, he wished everyone could just be like Tzarcyzk-616. He thought that guy was perfect. He watched him the most intently, marveling at his robotic cock as he pleasured Soo Soo. He was obviously doing the best job.

Everyone in the world should be robots, Guy thought.

And he continued watching, as the giant pyramid still hovered overhead. It kept zapping lazers in every direction as bodies mashed together in ecstasy. The lizard people fell, and the cacophony of death drowned out the moans of the group orgy below the great pyramid. And the group remained unseen beneath the all-seeing eye.

"Does anyone have a towel?" Nigel asked.

No. No one had a towel.

CHAPTER EIGHTEEN
BACK IN SPACE

Derf played with his pet Glyptodon, Derk. They frolicked in the sun, near Derf's cave. Derf was happy as could be. He was so happy to see his pet Glyptodon. It felt good to have the familiarity of home back again.

Then an alert rang out, and Derk sighed.

He went over to the wall console and shut off the program, and the hologram collapsed around him and folded itself away.

It looked as though the crew were back.

They would be happy to know that Derf got the ship back in shape and everything was running in perfect order.

When he got to the ship's entrance, the crew were pounding on the outside door. Derf looked out the window. The crew were all completely naked and all dirty, like they had been rolling around in the dirt together.

"DIRT!" Derf shouted.

He had just cleaned the whole entire ship. He used the ship's automated vacuums and floor polishers, but he still had programmed them and pushed all the buttons.

"LET US IN, DERF!" Guy yelled, pounding on the door.

Nigel corrected him.

"HIS NAME IS FRED!"

Derf looked past the group. Something was moving through the tree line at an incredible speed, crashing through the jungle, splintering wood.

The first thing Derf saw emerge through the jungle were tentacles. *BIG* tentacles.

"DERF!" Captain Paul shouted. "We are going *to die*. OPEN THE DOOR!"

"Aye, Captain!" Derf said, as if he was just awaiting the captain's orders and didn't take anyone else's.

Derf hit the button to open the door, and the crew piled in naked on top of him, all greasy and writhing around, panting and sweating.

It gave Derf a huge boner.

"CLOSE THE DOOR!" Captain Paul screamed.

And at that moment Derf could completely see what was coming out of the jungle. It was a 50-foot-tall pink monster covered in large tentacles, with big rows of teeth and spiked barbs and eight yellow eyes and all that shit.

It did not look like a penis at all. It looked like a gigantic squid. Even though it was pink, penises don't tend to be covered in teeth and barbs and have monstrous eyes.

A tentacle shot into the entrance and slapped Nigel on the ass.

"BLIMEY!" he shouted.

And then Derf finally slammed the control button and the door cut off the tentacle. The beast outside screeched, and the severed tentacle flopped around the hall like a dying fish.

Then the beast started bashing against the outside of the hull with its non-penis like appendages.

"DERF!" Derf screamed his own name for some reason, when he was really just upset that it was damaging the ship he had worked so hard to repair.

Paul stood, almost slipping and falling down because he was so greased up, but he caught himself.

"OK, CREW! Here's what we're going to do. Everybody fall in line."

Everybody stood up straight and awaited orders.

"Alright, first things first—we're all going to hit the showers. Then we're going to relax for a little bit and see what there is to wear, since we all lost our uniforms somehow."

"Counselor Soo," he addressed her appropriately.

"Yes, Captain?"

"Then you're going to take all those mushrooms to the galley so we can have them later."

She had two big bags full of the magic alien mushrooms she picked. Actually, she had just used two of their uniforms as a basket, tying the pant legs and sleeves together.

"Should I put them in the refrigerator?" she asked.

"I don't know what a refrigerator is, since I'm from 11th Century Norway and all. But, sure."

"And then what?" Commander Dickinson asked, as the beast still pounded away on the outside hull of the ship.

"Are we going to get rid of the monster outside,

maybe?" Guy sneered.

"Shut up, Guy," Paul said. "I was just getting to that. Lieutenant Tzarcyzk-616!" Paul shouted.

"Yes sir!"

"I want you to find out how to work the lazer cannons on the outside of the ship, and then explode the giant beast with the lazers. Can you do that? Shoot a bunch of big lazers at it somehow?"

"Aye aye, Captain!"

Tzarcyzk-616 smiled. It felt great to be such a valuable part of the crew. His knowledge of tech from the future where he's from was really starting to come in handy. Hell, he even went to lazer school when he was younger. He knows the correct spelling of the word and everything, including what it stands for.

He started writing that down on a note card so he could show someone later. He still had his pens and note cards.

"And Engineer Derf," Paul continued. "I assume that the Star Smasher is back in perfect working order and this boat is ready to get back into the air?"

Derf nodded.

"Derf make ship go."

"Excellent!" Paul smiled, happy that leaving the repairs to a caveman from the year 90,000 B.C. ended up working out so well.

"Alright, crew!" Paul clapped his hands together. "Let's hit the showers!"

"We're still going to do that first?" Guy asked.

"SHUT UP, GUY!" Paul shouted.

"Of course we're doing that first. We're all filthy dirty. And just look at Counselor Soo," he pointed to her. "We all came in her hair."

"Yeah," Nigel said. "Who knew that Frankenstein's cum would be so green?"

They all laughed, and even Frankenstein joined in. He definitely saw the humor in the situation.

"FRANKENSTEIN NOT DEAD!" he smiled.

"Hell no, you're not!" Nigel said, and raised his hand up to give Frankenstein a high-five.

"*RAAAA!*" Frankenstein roared at him.

Nigel took his hand down and stepped back immediately.

"OK," he said. "Never mind."

"Alright everyone," Paul said, as the beast continued its loud assault on the ship. "Enough standing around. Let's go!"

As they all went to leave the hall finally, Counselor Soo noticed the severed tentacle on the floor still squirming around.

"Wait a second," she said, picking it up off the ground. "I'm taking this with me. Let's go!"

Nigel smiled at her.

CHAPTER NINETEEN
THE EXPERIMENT

The crew sat around the bridge in comfortable robes, enjoying the hot cups of Earl Grey tea that Guy had poured for everybody.

"Tea time was *such* an excellent idea, Number One. I don't know why we never had it back in Norway. It would just be so, so..." Paul searched for the right word.

"*Civilised?*" Nigel asked, smiling a bit cockily.

"Probably!" Paul said.

Guy rolled his eyes.

"Alright, crew!" Paul said. "Let's get back to business."

Everyone settled into their stations like they were ready to get back to business.

"Number One."

"Yes, Captain?" Nigel asked.

"Status report!"w

"Aye aye, Captain."

Nigel picked his cup of tea back up, and said, "Lieutenant Commander Zarsh!"

Tzarcyzk-616 swung around in his swivel chair to face the commander, happy that he was apparently now *co*-commander, in addition to being a lieutenant.

"Yes, Commander Dickinson!"

"Read the status report!"

"Aye aye, sir!"

Tzarcyzk-616 got out his note cards and started going through them, reading them all one by one, to himself, but not out loud. It seemed very interesting to him. He kept going, "*Hmmmm!*" whenever he read something especially exciting.

Everyone watched him patiently, sipping their tea. Except for Counselor Soo, who became bored and got out her nail kit and started doing her nails.

"AHEM!" Nigel said, clearing his throat.

Tzarcyzk didn't look up from his note cards.

"AHEM! AHEM!" Nigel cleared his throat again, a little more obviously.

Tzarcyzk still didn't notice.

Nigel sighed, and turned to the captain.

"Anyway, Captain," he said. "The shower was lovely; we found clean robes, but no luck on finding new uniforms, so it looks like we're stuck with these, which is no problem since they are quite comfortable."

Captain Paul nodded.

"I agree! These are so nice I don't think we need those uniforms anymore anyway. I could wear this for the rest of my life."

"Agreed," Nigel continued. "Anyway, me and Counselor Soo went to the galley and rinsed off the mushrooms we found on Planet... let's call it *Planet X*, and then we put them in the refrigerator, which is a kind of cold cupboard that keeps food fresh, and then we both made love on the floor."

"Very good!" Paul nodded.

"We're going steady now, by the way," Nigel added.

"Meanwhile," he continued, "Lieutenant Commander Zarsh—I gave him the title of co-commander, by the way."

"Yes," Paul interjected. "I heard."

"He found the lazer cannon control room, and obliterated the pink monster outdoors attacking the ship while we all watched from the window."

"That was my favorite part!" Paul said.

"Yes, those lazers were quite something! Tzarcyzk-616 sure knows how to shoot a lazer beam!" Nigel said, excitedly.

"And then?" Paul asked.

"And then Derf got us back in space, and now we're flying away from Planet X."

Derf turned around in his swivel chair and made hand motions at the captain.

"Derf make ship go."

"Awesome!" Paul said.

"But where are we going?" Guy asked.

"SHUT UP, GUY!"

"YEAH GUY! PISS OFF!" Nigel added, but with a little British slang thrown in so you're reminded that he's British.

Guy put his head down, chagrined.

"Wait a second, Captain," Nigel said, looking over at him. "He's got a point."

Paul looked serious for a second, and worried.

"Where are we going?" the British butler said.

"I guess I always figured we would go home," Paul replied, staring out into the stars on the ship's viewscreen. They flew past them as beautiful white streaks. Paul was mesmerized by the starshine. But it made him sad.

"I have a whole life back there," he paused, and looked down. "But I don't know if I want to get back to it just yet."

"I have to get back," Papillon said. "I'm going to be shooting a movie soon."

"And Derf feed Derk. Derf miss Derk."

The caveman frowned.

"I'm just a simple butler back home though," Nigel said. "Out here I'm a commander, on a spaceship! I've made new friends and I think I've even finally met the right girl."

Papillon smiled at him.

Nigel looked back at Frankenstein, who was standing around like a useless paperweight as usual.

"How about you, Frankenstein? Do you even have a home to go back to?"

Frankenstein growled.

"Frankenstein Jew! Have no home."

Frankenstein pounded his fist on his tactical station, breaking the console completely.

Tzarcyzk-616 was furiously writing new note cards this whole time. They were maybe the most important ones yet. They were all about the ancient aliens, space ISIS, and why they were brought together in the first place, which everyone has seem to forgotten—the experiment!

"We're all from different points in time though," Paul reminded everybody. "Do we even know how to get home?"

At that moment, the man in the white lab coat suddenly appeared onscreen and looked at them with angry scowl.

"Oh, none of you are going *anywhere*. Did you all forget about me?"

"DOCTOR YES!" they all shouted in unison, suddenly remembering him.

"Doctor Yes? No! You can call me 'Y' from now on."

"Why 'Y', Y?" Guy asked.

"SHUT UP, GUY!" Y shouted.

"I just think it would be cool to have a one-letter name at this point in the story," Y said, suddenly looking embarrassed. "Uh, I mean *experiment*."

He composed himself, regaining his train of thought.

"Yes! Experiment! That's it! That's what I'm doing to you all!" he menaced them with his hands like an evil puppet master while he said that.

Everyone gasped. That was scary.

"I have taken you all out of your timelines, given you small doses of LSD, and thrown you all together on this warship that I stole!"

"But why, Y, why?!" Paul asked in a panic.

"I'm a psychiatrist!" Y said. "I must have a good reason!" He sounded like he didn't actually have a good reason.

"But no matter!" Y said. "Time to get back to it!"

Y snapped his fingers.

Straps shot out of their seats, ensnaring them all in the restraints.

"CAPTAIN!" Nigel shouted. "I CAN'T BREAK FREE!"

"Nor can I, Number One! And it seems like there isn't a thing we can do about it!"

"LIEUTENANT COMMANDER TZARCYZK!" Paul shouted. "IS THERE ANYTHING WE CAN DO ABOUT IT?!"

"No!" Tzarcyzk shouted back at him.

"I didn't think so," Paul said, looking back at Nigel.

And then panels opened on the ceiling, and terrifying metal devices covered in mechanical arms and wires descended, covering each crew member below. The wires wrapped around their bodies as metal pincers held open their eyes and mouths and needles and blades whirled around in front of their faces.

"And now..." Y clasped his hands together. "The next phase."

They all tried to scream, but their screams were muffled by the anti-screaming instruments of the devices, which went straight into their mouths to prevent screams.

The needles dripped with fluid, ready to penetrate.

"You will be given a much higher dose of LSD this time. But in addition to a higher dose, it contains new ingredients that you happened to gather from what you called *Planet X*, on your little excursion there."

The mushrooms! Paul thought.

"But I have mutated them into an evolved crystalline form, and intensified its psychotropic properties, for *nefarious* reasons!" Y grinned. "And now you shall all experience the full effects of that!"

Y cocked an eyebrow at them. "Through *the eyes!*"

Everyone tried to scream as the needles shot straight into their eyeballs and injected them with liquid acid. They bled from their eyes and convulsed.

Y snapped his fingers.

The devices let them all go and retracted back into the ceiling. Then their restraints unstrapped suddenly and they were free.

Everyone rubbed their eyes, some of them moaning in pain and rolling around on the floor, and others screaming in blinded terror.

But not Captain Paul. He stood up immediately and faced Y, looking at him with a vengeance.

"Oh, a challenger," Y noted, and smiled. "*Good.*"

Paul fixed his eyes on the mad scientist and didn't back down.

"You're the one I've watched the most. Paul, the primitive Viking warrior. Such a good leader. Such a presence. And so *adaptable.*"

Y snapped his fingers again, and the ship rumbled and the bridge shook violently. They were being shot through space and time at such an incredible speed that it warped the air around them and made cool tracers and light flares appear all over.

"*Oooooh!*" the whole crew thought.

And then the ship came to a screeching halt.

Not strapped in, Tzarcyzk-616 flew straight over his console head first into the wall. Frankenstein stumbled and tripped over him, twisting his ankle. He roared.

Sparks flew out of the computer system and little fires started all over.

Paul still stood where he was standing. He stood tall, a stoic figure. A pillar of strength. All those admirable things you'd come to expect from a Viking. He had kept his eyes fixed on Y. He hadn't moved an inch the whole time.

Y sneered at him one last time.

"Adapt to *this!*"

He pressed a button on his computer and disappeared from the screen, automatically reverting it to space view so they could all see what was ahead of the ship.

An enormous space station hung there, bigger than three Planet X's, like it was XXX sized, and a squadron of large scimitar-shaped starships hovered in front of it, facing them.

The ships' lazer cannons all started glowing red.

"THEY'RE CHARGING LAZERS!" Commander Dickinson shouted.

"Those look awesome!" Guy said. "WOW!"

"SHIELDS UP!" Paul commanded. "ALL HANDS TO BATTLE STATIONS!"

Captain Paul sat back in his captain's chair.

He was determined.

He was going to put a stop to Space ISIS once and for all.

CHAPTER TWENTY
SPACE ISIS

Deadly lazers exploded from the cannons of the ISIS warships. Awesome sound effects rang out through space. Don't listen to anyone when they tell you it's impossible for sound to travel through the vacuum of outer space. That's bullshit. You can totally hear it. If anything, lazer sounds are even *more* awesome in space. They're totally amplified.

The crew of the S.S. Mashrue, better known as the *Star Smasher*, could especially hear the sound of amplified lazer beams shooting through space. The effects of the psychedelics were gripping them so hard that they could not only *hear* the lazer beams from inside their ship, but they could *feel* them, and even taste them.

Red lazer beams tasted like *Spree,* the light and lively candy. Some of them had never tried Spree, of course, being from the wrong era of time to enjoy them, but if they ever did someday enjoy a piece of Spree candy, they would think, *Mmmmm, this tastes like lazers.*

"RAISE SHIELDS!" the captain commanded.

Derf was using the controls on the console with his feet, as if he'd got his legs confused with his arms. He hit the button with his big toe just in time, and the lazers that were about to hit the ship and explode it to pieces slid off the forward shield and dissipated into space around them. It was such a beautiful display of color onscreen. It was as if it hit their windshield like a bug and was sprayed off with Kool-Aid instead of wiper fluid. This had the crew dazzled once more.

I wish I had a pair of 3D glasses, Nigel wished.

But Paul was not dazzled, he was pissed.

"They're charging their lazers again! Take evasive actions!"

Guy turned over Tzarcyzk-616, who appeared to be lying there lifeless next to his console. He screamed when he saw his face. It was missing half of its skin and metallic bone shined and sparked with blue electricity. Tzarcyzk's eye hung out of its socket by red cables. It was like he was dead.

But then Tzarcyzk reached up and grabbed Guy by the arm, with his skeletal robot hand that had had its skin burnt off to reveal the metal framework below.

Guy screamed his head off and tried to get away, trying to force Tzarcyzk to relinquish his grip. The alien's face still appeared lifeless, and the mouth didn't even move when it said, "*HELP ME.*"

This was too much for Guy to handle on acid. He passed out.

When he woke up, Tzarcyzk-616 was still working at his console, like nothing had happened.

He looked Guy's way, and thought at him, *Here we are again, Guy Mann.*

"Tzarcyzk!" Guy shouted. "You're alive! What happened?"

When the lazers hit the ship...

"Yes?!"

I'm sorry, Guy... but you didn't make it.

Guy fell to his knees and screamed, "*NOOOOOO!*"

Then he heard Tzarcyzk laughing.

Relax, Guy. I'm just kidding.

"What?" Guy asked. "I'm not dead?"

Of course not. I just linked up to your mind when you became unconscious. This is why I'm in your head. Now, I need you to do something for me, Guy.

"Anything! How can I help?"

I need you to reboot me.

"No problem, man! How do I do it?"

My penis is actually an on/off switch. I need you to grab it, and pull on it again and again until I restart. This may take several tries. Yank as hard as you can, and keep up a good motion. Don't let go.

"Are you fucking kidding me?" Guy asked.

Of course not. Please, Guy. Our lives depend on it. You're our only hope.

"OK," Guy said. "If I'm our only hope, I guess."

Good. Now turn me on.

Guy suddenly woke up, and without hesitation, pulled Tzarcyzk-616's robotic cock out of his pants and started yanking on it.

"GUY!" the captain shouted. "WHY ARE YOU JERKING OFF LIEUTENANT COMMANDER TZARCYZK!?"

Guy smiled.

"Don't worry, Captain! It's the only way to bring him back to life!"

"AH! KEEP AT IT THEN! PULL HARDER!"

"I'M GIVING IT ALL I'VE GOT, CAPTAIN!" Guy shouted.

And with that, Tzarcyzk sat up, suddenly awake.

"Thank you, Guy. I seem to be fully functional again."

Guy noticed a dark blue fluid running down his arm, and a big wet spot of it on his robe.

"UGH!" Guy screamed. "Alien robot jizz! It's all over me!"

Paul came over and touched some with his finger, then put his finger in his mouth.

"Mmmmm," he moaned. "Tastes like lingonberries."

"OH MY GOD!" Guy yelped. "IS THIS EVEN HAPPENING!? I AM TRIPPING THE FUCK OUT RIGHT NOW!"

"I knew he couldn't handle his shit," Nigel said to the captain, who was sitting right next to him the whole time.

Tzarcyzk got back in his pilot's chair.

"TAKE EVASIVE ACTIONS!" Paul commanded.

Déjà vu! Nigel thought. *Didn't the captain just say that a while ago? Oh my, I hope we're not trapped in some kind of time loop. That must be it. We're trapped in some kind of time loop. Oh well, I'll just sit back and enjoy the ruddy ride.*

Nigel crossed his legs and poured a cup of Earl Grey tea and took a sip.

Tzarcyzk got ready to take evasive actions on the controls.

"But Captain..." he said. "They're not shooting anything at us right now for us to dodge."

"WELL GET READY FOR IT!"

"AYE AYE, CAPTAIN!"

"Their lazers seem to take an awfully long time to charge," Nigel noted, sipping his tea. "Don't you think, Captain?"

Nigel turned to him, but only saw a big fluffy white rabbit, like the Easter Bunny. It turned to him and flashed a mouthful of sharp pointy teeth. Nigel screamed and dropped his tea.

"YES, NUMBER ONE!" Paul said from across the room near the viewscreen. "Their lazers seem to take a long time to recharge. You can see their cannons glowing more and more red, but they seem to not be anywhere near climaxing yet. Perhaps we could use this weakness to our advantage somehow."

Frankenstein growled.

"FRANKENSTEIN! HURT!"

"Oh yeah, Gay Guy!" Paul said.

"HEY!" Guy objected.

"Sorry, I mean *Doctor* Gay Guy," Paul snickered. "Make yourself useful and bandage Frankenstein's ankle up."

Guy sighed and said, "*Fine.*"

"And try not to jerk him off while you're at it."

"There's probably no time for that now," Nigel said to Counselor Soo, sipping another hot cup of tea.

But when he looked over to her she was nothing but a plastic blowup doll, with red pouty lips and big plastic breasts.

"*Me love you long time,*" it said to him.

Nigel screamed and threw his teacup in the air, and hot tea went everywhere. Then he poured another cup and started blowing on it, still looking at the blowup doll, which he ended up deciding was pretty hot and tried to start a conversation with it.

Papillon later came back from the bathroom, and caught Nigel fucking the blowup doll in her seat, making big, squeaky sounds.

"NIGEL!" she shouted.

Papillon had just put the doll there because she didn't want anyone to know she was gone during such a crucial moment.

"Hey baby, care to join us?" Nigel asked her with a smile.

"NO!!!!" she protested.

Then she thought about it, and said, "OK, maybe."

She opened up her robe and put her breasts in Nigel's face, and he sucked on them while he squeakily fucked the plastic blow up doll.

"OK GUYS! THOSE LAZERS ARE CHARGING UP! THIS IS GETTING SERIOUS NOW! EVERYONE TAKE THEIR POSITIONS!" Paul commanded.

Half of the crew were having sex and the other half were tripping out over minor things in the room and one of them might have even been on fire.

Paul pointed his finger at the ship's viewscreen. "ENGAGE!"

The deadly lazer explodathon hit the S.S. Mashrue with full force.

CHAPTER TWENTY-ONE
DEADLY LAZER
EXPLODATHON

"SHIELDS AT 100%, CAPTAIN!" Lieutenant Fred shouted, fully evolved and no longer looking like a caveman.

"That's good, right? 100%. That's got to be good," Guy noted.

"SHUT UP, GUY!"

The captain sighed; the crew was falling apart all of a sudden. His ship's counselor and second-in-command were having a cigarette after they shagged, and you can't even smoke on a starship because you'd supposedly explode, and his first helmsman was apparently caught in a wild *timestorm*, which caused him to evolve millions of years in a matter of seconds.

Captain Paul knew all of this because it said so on the note card that Tzarcyzk just handed him.

And he just ran up and handed him another one.

He's reading that upside down; he actually means that the shields are at 001%.

"BY ODIN'S BEARD!" Paul shouted.

A million red lazer beams were heading right for them.

"They'll cut through us like nothing!"

Tzarcyzk ran up with another note card.

Captain, I have an idea.

Paul struck the card out of his hand.

"Dammit, man, just tell me!"

"OK," Tzarcyzk said, as confident as a professional speaker. "I think if I isolate the timestorm around Lieutenant Derf, I can use it to reverse the polarities of the enemy lazers, not only slowing them down to a crawl before they hit us, but if I get the calculations *just right* I think I can reverse the direction the lazer beams are heading in, speed them up, and shoot them back at ISIS!"

"Alright, man! Now you're thinking!" Paul said.

And then he put his hand on his shoulder and complimented him.

"And you sounded as confident as a professional speaker, Tzarcyzk-616. I am proud of you."

Tzarcyzk smiled. It was all he ever wanted— to make someone proud of him. When you're an alien robot from the future, you're expected to do your job, and there's no reward for doing it. You just do it.

"Now, everyone return to their seats! Tzarcyzk, start calculating! Let's put that timestorm between us and ISIS ASAP!"

Paul looked over to Papillon and Nigel.

"And you two! Put your robes back on! And put out those cigarettes! This is a non-smoking spaceship!"

"HA!" Guy taunted them. "You got yelled at!"

"SHUT UP, GUY! Go make sure Frankenstein can stand up straight."

"HEY!" Guy grumbled. "OK, fine..."

"I think I might be able to put him to good use soon..." Paul said, thinking up a plan.

"LIEUTENANT COMMANDER? ARE YOU READY?"

"YES SIR!"

"FIRE AT WILL!"

Tzarcyzk pressed a bunch of buttons on his computer console at lightning fast speed and it sent the timestorm out in front of them, captured the lazers, and slowed them down to a crawl, just like he calculated.

And when they seemed like they were not moving at all, frozen for a split second in space, the lazers rocketed back to where they came from—straight at the squadron of ISIS ships, exploding them right out spacetime in an instant!

It lit up the viewscreen brightly like a bright fireworks display and everyone cheered! The deadly lazer explodathon went off in full effect, and the squadron of ISIS starships had been destroyed, lazer blasted to smithereens. It was beautiful.

"WAY TO GO, TEAM!" Captain Paul said.

Everyone jumped up and down with excitement, gave each other high-fives, kissed, and everything. Even Guy patted Tzarcyzk on the shoulder, smiled, and gave it a little squeeze. Tzarcyzk smiled back.

Frankenstein walked out into the middle of the crowd with his arms outstretched and started moving back and forth, and spinning around, shifting side to side.

"What's Frankenstein doing?" Nigel asked.

"I think he's doing a dance!" Papillon replied with excitement.

"GO, FRANKENSTEIN, GO!" Nigel hollered.

But Frankenstein wasn't doing a dance. He was trapped in the timestorm.

"TIMESTORM! RAAAAA!" Frankenstein growled.

"Lieutenant Commander!" Captain Paul shouted. "What is happening to Frankenstein?"

Tzarcyzk checked the readings on his computer.

"A little piece of the timestorm must have shifted across the bridge while I moved it away from Derf."

Captain Paul looked over at Derf. He was just a skeleton now, slumped over his console.

"BY ODIN'S BEARD!" Paul yelled. "HE'S BEEN TURNED INTO A SKELETON!"

"I could possibly turn him back if I got the timestorm away from Frankenstein!"

"Then do it, man! People are dying!"

Frankenstein held his temples and screamed.

"TIMESTORM... *HURT!*"

The crew watched helplessly as the timestorm slowly turned Frankenstein's green skin back into a healthy shade of white.

"Far out, man!" Papillon said, mesmerized.

"Wait, this is good, right?" Paul asked Nigel. "This will turn him back into a human being."

Nigel shook his head.

"No, Captain, this is bad."

Frankenstein howled in agony as his stitches

became undone. The bolts on his head popped out and rocketed across the room in opposite directions, shattering glass panels on the walls. One of his arms fell off. And another.

"He's falling apart!" Papillon said.

"FRANKENSTEIN... *DYING!*" he screamed.

And then his head fell off. It bounced when it hit the floor.

"BY ODIN'S BEARD!" Captain Paul yelled.

Tzarcyzk-616 sat at his console, writing down other Viking phrases that a Norsemen might say other than *BY ODIN'S BEARD!*, and planned to show Paul the card as soon as he had some free time.

Frankenstein's legs walked a few feet before they fell over. One separated at the knee, and the other rolled off at the thigh. And then Frankenstein's penis fell off.

Papillon took Frankenstein's robe off the floor and threw it on his penis to cover it.

But then Frankenstein's body parts started growing. Not in size, but they were regenerating from the stumps of where they had been cut off of the original dead bodies.

"*Oh no...*" Nigel said.

"Number One! What is happening?" Paul asked.

"Well," Nigel began, "Frankenstein was made up of dead body parts, and wait... did I mention this already, or am I stuck in a timeloop? I can't really tell."

"Just continue."

"Alrighty then, Frankenstein is reversing,

coming back to life. Or rather—the people who he was made up of are coming back to life. In a few minutes, they'll be fully regenerated and become the human beings they once were before death."

"BY ODIN'S—"

Tzarcyzk-616 interrupted Paul, and handed him a note card of various Viking phrases and slang. He pointed to one of his favorites.

"Really? That one?" Paul asked him.

Tzarcyzk nodded.

"OK, maybe I'll try it later. Thank you, Lieutenant Commander."

Tzarcyzk smiled.

Papillon screamed.

"THEY'RE GROWING BIGGER AND BIGGER! THEY'LL BECOME MONSTROSITIES! THEY'LL KILL US ALL! OH MY GOD, I CAN'T TAKE IT ANYMORE!"

Papillon grabbed a lazer rifle.

"I'LL KILL THEM ALL! ME MURDER YOU LONG TIME!"

"Papillon, no!" Paul shouted.

Nigel pressed down on the barrel, and she lowered the rifle. He took her in his arms. He patted her on the back.

"There, there. It's OK."

She buried her face in his manly chest hair, sticking out of his robe, which is what they were all still wearing, and she cried.

"Captain," Nigel asked. "Permission to leave the bridge?"

Paul sighed.

"Permission granted."

They took their leave, and Papillon whimpered.

"I just can't take it anymore, it's too horrifying."

"I know! And he doesn't do anything for like, *ever*, and then he goes and pulls all that? Bad show."

Nigel smiled at her.

"Let's go find Sun Ra!"

Papillon's face lit up.

"Sun Ra?! YAY!"

"C'mon, baby," Nigel said, "maybe he'll take us for a ride on his rocket ship, and take us away from this place."

Back on the bridge, the rest of the crew watched as Frankenstein's dead body parts grew and came back to life.

"They're missing out," Guy said, kicked back and relaxed in his chair, eating a bar of non-GMO tofu he found in the galley. "This is the exact kind of trippy stuff I like to watch on acid. It's like claymation or something, but in real life."

Guy was a little surprised the captain didn't tell him to shut up that time.

But Paul was fixated on the reanimation. He knew that when the severed limbs finally came back to life, he might just have a problem with them, and he would have to be ready.

By the time the limbs were almost done growing into full people, Papillon and Nigel arrived back on the bridge.

"Uh..." Papillon said, looking a little embarrassed.

"We got bored."

They took their seats next to the captain.

Nigel started tripping out on one as it grew eyes, ears, and a mouth. He was mesmerized by it, and as soon as it was finished growing a full face, he started applauding excitedly.

"Jolly good show!" he said.

"Be on the ready," Captain Paul said.

They were done growing, and seven completely reborn human beings stood before them, naked. They all looked very Eastern Bloc European.

"Where are we?" one asked.

"What happened? I was just out for a jog, when... *Oh my god*," another said.

"Hey guys!" the one who grew out of Frankenstein's head greeted, and waved.

"I remember everything. Thanks for trying to help, but the timestorm freed me from that monstrous prison. It was just what I needed!"

New Frankenstein smiled. He was actually quite a handsome man.

"But wait," Nigel said. "There were *eight* body parts. But there are only seven people. Where is the eighth? Where is Frankenstein's *penis*?"

"Oh," Papillon said. "I covered it with a robe."

Then she pointed.

"It's standing right over there."

A figure was standing covered with a robe.

"BY ODIN'S BEARD!" Paul said.

Tzarcyzk sighed, and shook his head at him.

"GUY!"

"Yes, Captain?"

"Go take that robe off of that guy. Let's see who we have here."

"Aye aye, Captain."

Guy went up to the robe and pulled it off, only to reveal...

"ADOLF HITLER!?!?!" Guy screamed.

"SIEG HEIL!" Adolf yelled, and put his hands around Guy's neck and started strangling him.

And there he was, Adolf Hitler, standing there naked, with his fully formed Charlie Chaplin moustache and everything.

New Frankenstein screamed in shock, but in a less monstrous way since he was human now.

"My penis was... *Adolf Hitler!?*"

"Who is Adolf Hitler?" Captain Paul asked.

"Oh, Hitler was a political leader in Germany from Frankenstein's era," Nigel informed him. "He was responsible for the genocide of six million Jews. He's a very rotten man."

"BY ODIN'S BEARD!" Paul shouted. "THAT'S TERRIBLE!"

"So, you mean the whole time I was with Frankenstein," Papillon wondered, "his penis was Adolf Hitler?"

"No honey, that would be ridiculous," Nigel said.

Papillon let out a sigh of relief.

"Frankenstein's penis *was* Adolf Hitler's penis."

"You mean I had Adolf Hitler's dick in my mouth?" Papillon asked.

"Unfortunately, yes."

Papillon leaned over her chair and puked.

Captain Paul let Hitler choke Guy for a little while longer, and then shouted, "OK, NEW CREW! GRAB ADOLF HITLER!"

The seven newly reborn bodies complied, kind of keen with what was going on. They all knew about Adolf Hitler, of course.

"But how did Adolf Hitler get his penis sewn onto my body?" New Frankenstein asked.

"IT WAS MY PLAN ALL ALONG, YOU FOOL!" Adolf Hitler yelled.

"But you weren't even dead when I was created. And I just fought you all winter. And I even saw you taking a leak once. You still had a penis."

"Oh, Frankenstein," Hitler taunted. "Timestorms can do wondrous things!"

Then an alarm blared and the whole ship started shaking.

"EVERYONE BACK TO THEIR BATTLE STATIONS!" Paul commanded.

And then he further commanded, "FRANKENSTEIN! TAKE ADOLF HITLER TO THE BRIG!"

"AYE AYE, CAPTAIN!" New Frankenstein responded.

"Papillon, get all these naked men some robes!"

"AYE AYE, CAPTAIN!"

"TZARCYZK-616! ON SCREEN!"

"AYE AYE, CAPTAIN!"

Tzarcyzk flipped on the ship's viewscreen as the bridge rumbled and shook.

The gigantic ISIS space station that everyone had forgotten about, which was at least the size of three planets, had them gripped in a tractor beam.

"BY ODIN'S BEARD!" Paul shouted, *again*. "I forgot about that thing!"

"It's Planet XXX!" Tzarcyzk confirmed. "It's pulling us in! I can't break us free, Captain! And I'm giving it all she's got!"

"Oh wait, I think I can do it," Derf said, pulling back on the controls. "I'm not a skeleton anymore."

"Way to go, caveman!" Paul shouted.

"Oh wait, never mind. I can't do it. The pull is too strong. We're getting sucked in."

Captain Paul stood and looked at the space station that was pulling them in.

"It's... *massive*."

"Alright, what do we do?" Paul addressed his crew. "Any suggestions? Counselor Soo?"

"Well, Captain," she answered. "Since we're all under the influence of Y's psychotropical experiment, I would say that none of this is probably happening at all and we should just wait it out and enjoy the trip."

"Wrong," Paul said. "This is definitely happening. I built up an immunity to Y's nefarious drugs and have not been under the influence of them this entire time. I have been clear minded."

He pointed over to Tzarcyzk-616.

"And so has he."

"The captain is correct. The drugs cannot affect me. They never have. I have always been immune."

"Oh, OK," Papillon said. "But I'm sure we can all agree that timestorm was pretty trippy though."

"Yeah," Paul smiled. "That was pretty cool."

"Anyway, once the Star Smasher has been pulled completely inside, we will probably be boarded. This used to happen to me and my men a lot whenever we sailed through Russia. Those Russians... they're dicks."

"Captain..."

"Yes, Number One?"

"I think I might have an idea..."

CHAPTER TWENTY-TWO
NIGEL'S PLAN

"Wait, never mind. I actually can't think of anything. I *thought* I did. Something that starts with a *B*? A plan B?" Nigel wondered.

"GODDAMNIT, NIGEL!" Captain Paul shouted. "You need to bring your *A* game to your plan *B*!"

Nigel looked perturbed.

"I don't think I know what you're talking about, Captain."

"Yeah," Paul responded. "Neither do I."

They were approaching Planet XXX, trapped in its thrall. A big hatch opened, and they were heading straight towards it.

"Oh well, here we go," Paul sighed, defeated. "I guess we'll just *give up!*" He threw his hands up in the air.

"Wait!" Nigel shouted.

"What?"

"I *do* have an idea!"

"Alright, man! Let's hear it!"

"What if we wrapped our robes around our heads like turbans, and pretended we were members of ISIS too?"

"That's fucking stupid!" Paul said, dismissively.

"Well then I don't know!"

"We'd all be naked!"

"Well it'd be better to be naked than to be dead!" Nigel countered.

"This is the worst acid trip ever," Guy said, folding his arms in disappointment.

The S.S. Mashrue was fully inside the Planet XXX star station, or whatever it was. Some kind of star that shot lazers. A sort of star of... *death*.

The Death Star closed its bay doors and the S.S. Mashrue was trapped inside.

It's not a Death Star! Guy heard someone scream in his mind.

"WHO WAS THAT?!" he asked, flipping out.

"SHUT UP, GUY!" Captain Paul said. "Alright everyone, I have an idea. It's so crazy, it just might work! Take off your robes and wrap them around your heads. We're going to play ISIS."

Nigel sighed, and started to disrobe.

"Well, I guess *everyone's* seen my penis at this point."

"We haven't," said one of Frankenstein's body part donors.

"Yeah," said another one. "It's really small."

Oh, blimey, Nigel thought. *Here we go again.*

"Is anyone ever going to explain to us what is going on?" another Frankenstein man asked, standing around bewildered.

No one answered him. It was too hard to explain.

"Alright, now everyone grab a lazer rifle and follow me out to the ship's entrance in the bay downstairs, or whatever you call it, this ship is confusing," Paul said.

"When the terrorists board us, I want you all to follow my lead."

The crew all nodded.

"Alright, team! Let's go!"

Paul tried to count how many crew members he now had total, but math was never his strong suit. *Twenty-three?* That seemed like a good number. Yeah, twenty-three.

CHAPTER TWENTY-THREE
SPACE ISIS BOARDS THE SHIP

The door blew off its hinges, exploded by the force of a deadly lazer blast.

It flew straight at Paul. He blocked it with one of Frankenstein's body donors, who instantly became a bloody lifeless pulp.

"Alright team," Paul commanded. "Everyone grab a Frankenstein! Use it as a human shield! And fire at will!"

ISIS terrorists poured into the hallway, ululating their battle cry, "*LA ILAH ELA ALLAH!*"

The hall filled with red lazer blasts, coming straight at the crew. Everyone held their Frankenstein right up in front of them as a full body shield and each shield took the full brunt of the blasts and died. The crew returned fire, and their lazer rifles shot out *blue* lazer blasts, so you could tell the good guys' lazer beams from the bad guys' lazer beams.

"Hey!" said Guy. "This reminds me of something!"

"What, Guy?" Nigel asked, sarcastically. "*Star Wars? Star Trek?* Any Frankenstein movie? *Time Bandits?* Hell, take your bloody pick!"

Yeah, Guy thought. *All of that.*

When the smoke cleared and every ISIS terrorist who had broken in were slaughtered, the team decided to leave the ship and check to see what was outside.

"Follow my lead, crew," Paul said. "Lazer guns at the ready."

"Why aren't you using that lazer sword you liked?" Tzarcyzk asked.

"Because I forgot all about it," Paul replied, and then looked at him crossly. "*Geez*, Tzar, *thanks for reminding me.* I would love to have that right now."

"You're welcome," Tzarcyzk-616 smiled back at him.

"Hey guys," New Frankenstein said. "Thanks for not using me as a human shield too. That was really nice of you."

"Of course, Frankenstein!" Papillon said. "You're the best!"

"Thank you, Counselor Soo!" the white monster smiled.

Paul tried to do the math in his head of how many crew members he had use human Frankenstein shields and if it all evened out, but he decided to forget about it. He was sure that all of his original crew had survived and that's all that mattered.

As they left the hall, Derf's unnoticed skeleton lay left behind, still clutching his lazer rifle.

CHAPTER TWENTY-FOUR
PLANET XXX

The gigantic spaceship hangar where the ship
had been pulled in was empty. There were no
guards or anyone waiting outside for them. Paul
wondered for a second if they had killed their
whole entire crew. Like, all that was left of the
ISIS space empire were those dozen or so men
they had just left dead aboard their ship.

"Lieutenant Commander Tzarcyzk," Captain
Paul said, in the official captain-like manner.

"Yes, Captain?"

"Can you scan this space station for life signs?"

"Can do, Captain."

Tzarcyzk-616 closed his eyes, as if he was
scanning the whole entire station with his
computer brain.

He opened his eyes.

"Done."

"Well?"

"There are only 7 life signs aboard this space
station. And those are ours."

"Wow, really?!" Paul said, astounded. "You
mean we just slaughtered what remained of ISIS?
We exploded all their stupid little ships and then
we just killed the last of their men? Like, they

pulled us into their space station and they figured the last remaining survivors of their people could take us, so they all went in at once?"

Paul started laughing his ass off.

"Man, that is classic! We wore turbans and everything! Hahaha! That rules."

"Or, you know, it still could not all be happening," Papillon said.

"You know, I gotta agree with her this time," Guy said. "This all seems like it's a little too convenient."

"Oh, pish posh!" Nigel said, dismissively. "We've already established that we're not hallucinating."

"*Really?*" Guy asked. "And with everything that happened with Frankenstein?"

"Bloody hell, kid, have you even been here the whole time?! This whole fucking story has been off-the-wall full-on *insane*. So enough already!"

Guy looked down, all miffed again.

"OK, crew—roll call!" Captain Paul said. "I've been doing the numbers in my head, and I'm a little bad with arithmetic, so everyone help me out here a little. Lieutenant Commander, you said there are only seven life signs aboard this vessel, correct?"

"Correct, Captain!" Tzarcyzk confirmed.

"Alright then, here we go—Commander Dickinson, you're Number One."

"Thank you, Captain," Nigel smiled.

"Me, I'll be number two," the captain said, holding out a second finger so he could keep count.

"Counselor Soo, you're number three. Gay Guy..."

"HEY!"

"...you're number four. Lieutenant Commander Tzarcyzk, you're number *five*..."

Captain Paul continued the count on his other hand.

"New Frankenstein, you're number six... and Engineer Derf, or Lieutenant Fred, or whoever, he'd be number seven, but hey..."

Captain Paul looked around.

"Where is he?"

"He's still back on the ship, I believe," Nigel speculated.

"So, he would account for the seventh life sign, right?" Paul asked.

"Correct."

But Derf didn't account for the last life sign. Unbeknownst to the crew, Derf had been skeletonized by a lazer blast in their final battle with ISIS.

The last life sign on board belonged to...
ADOLF HITLER!

CHAPTER TWENTY-FIVE
ADOLF HITLER

Adolf Hitler was locked up in the brig. He couldn't get out. It was pretty frustrating for him. He moped around thinking, *this isn't fair!* But he thought that in German since that was his first language. The words "this isn't fair" probably just sounded like *"SIEG HEIL!"* in German. So, Hitler probably just paced around the room thinking, *SIEG HEIL*, the whole time, over and over again. It was probably all that German Nazis thought about, all the time, and who even knows what it means? It could mean anything. A German is hungry, so he thinks *SIEG HEIL!* He liked a book, so he shouts *SIEG HEIL!* He's late to work, so, goddamn it, it's just *SIEG HEIL* all over again.

But then Adolf Hitler just thought about a bunch of other things, and it proved that he wasn't just thinking *SIEG HEIL* the whole time. The cell he was in had some kind of *lazer* wall. So, he was kind of terrified of that. He was from the 1940s. They didn't even have microwave ovens yet. He'd never even seen *Star Wars*, poor asshole. He would have loved it because he loved absolutely everything to do with wars. Well, not the bunker stuff. The bunker stuff sucked. But everything pre-bunker, SIEG FUCKING HEIL!

Then a man in a white laboratory coat suddenly appeared from out of nowhere, and stood outside his cell.

"SIEG HEIL!" Hitler shouted, horribly startled.

"Adolf Hitler. *Well well well...*" the man in the white lab coat said.

"Sieg heil?" Hitler asked, squinting through the lazer wall to see the man.

"Let me turn this off right here," the man said, and the lazer wall disappeared.

The man had a wild shock of white hair. He held up an ominous syringe, which he brandished nefariously.

"Josef Mengele?" Hitler asked.

"No, not Josef Mengele," the man in the white labcoat said. "You can call me *Doctor Yes*."

"*Nein!*" Hitler said.

"No, not Doctor *Nein*, Doctor *Yes*."

"Doctor *Ja?*" Hitler said.

"Christ, you couldn't *be* more German," Doctor Yes rolled his eyes, having had enough of Hitler's German nonsense.

"Look," Doctor Yes said, pointing to the needle. "This is a special brand of *super meth* that I whipped up just for you. It's going to make you invincible. After I inject you with it, I want you to find the crew of the S.S. Mashrue, and *destroy them!*"

"What's in it for me?" Hitler asked, as if he were in a position to make demands.

"You're in no position to make demands, *Adolf*

Hitler. But alright, if you carry out this task, I'll let you in on a little secret. A secret that might change the course of history and lead you to conquer *the world...*"

"Sieg Heil?" Hitler said, excitedly.

"*Ja,*" Doctor Yes said, putting his arm around Hitler's shoulders. "Just imagine it. *Planet Hitler!*"

Doctor Yes pointed out the words in the space in front of them as if they were written on a marquee.

"Planet *Hitler?*" Adolf's eyes widened, and he smiled. "*Ja!* This is good."

"Then we have a deal."

Doctor Yes put Hitler in a headlock and injected his nefarious syringe into the *Führer's* neck. *Führer* was apparently a word for a German man or superman or something. He let Hitler go.

Hitler screamed. His eyes instantly became bloodshot as his pupils dilated. He tore at his own clothes, making them tattered. The cords on his neck tensed as a vehement power coursed through his veins, which throbbed beneath his skin and bulged out.

"*BEHOLD!*" said Doctor Yes, all mad scientist-like. "*SUPER HITLER!*"

Super Hitler roared, and took off running down the hall like a wild beast.

"Yes! Run, my Hitler! Run! Destroy them all!"

Doctor Yes clasped his hands together, threw back his head, and cackled.

Then he stopped and a perturbed look changed his face.

"Why... why am I so evil?" he pondered, as if confused by his actions.

An ancient alien watched him from a viewscreen. It rubbed its hands together, saying with delight...

"*Yesssss... pull the strings... PULL THE STRINGS!*"

It laughed evilly. And then Doctor Yes just started laughing evilly too. Not knowing he was sharing it with someone.

CHAPTER TWENTY-SIX
SPACE ISIS RETURNS

"Well, that would explain everything."

Guy said, agreeing with Tzarcyzk's theory on the alien race that had destroyed Portland in the future.

Tzarcyzk-616 smiled. He had solved the mysteries of what was behind the upcoming climax, and had it all written out on a series of note cards with all the pertinent information, including spoilers, and not-to-be-believed conspiracy theories that he had just mathematically proven were true, such as *2 + 2 = ISIS!*

"I think I'll show these to the captain soon..." Guy said, taking the note cards away from him. "I'll just put these in my robe pocket for safe keeping..."

Guy planned to pass these cards off as his own and take all the credit.

What a douchebag, Tzarcyzk thought. *And I can't believe he's actually naïve enough to think Captain Paul would fall for that. He knows that I'm the one who writes important note cards for him to read. He probably even knows my handwriting by now. For Guy to think that the captain is so stupid...*

Tzarcyzk paused for a second, and thought, *You know what? That's it. I'm done. Fuck this Guy.*

He turned to walk away.

Captain Paul returned with Commander Dickinson and New Frankenstein.

"Did you guys have any luck?" Counselor Soo asked.

"No," Commander Dickinson responded. "We looked everywhere but we didn't find any new uniforms or clothing here whatsoever."

He put his hands in his robe pockets.

"I guess we're just stuck with these robes forever."

"Well," Captain Paul said, "at least they're nice."

Everyone agreed. It didn't seem to be that big a deal that they were stuck in robes for now until the foreseeable future.

"Anyone else find anything while we were gone?" Captain Paul asked.

"*Ooooh!*" Guy said, raising his hand.

Captain Paul rolled his eyes.

"OK, Guy, let's see what it is."

Guy ran up to Captain Paul and handed him the note cards.

"I figured it all out!" he said.

Captain Paul grabbed the note cards and started reading them.

"Mmmm-hmmm," he said. "*Ancient aliens,* very good. ISIS, the Illuminati, Adolf Hitler, the city of Portland... *uh-huh,* yes, I see how that all ties in here..."

Guy beamed.

"Yes, Captain, using my *superior intellect,* I was able to discern which theories were actually *bullshit,* and which ones were real."

Captain Paul read on, silently, and then looked back up at Guy.

"And all this about Doctor Yes... I mean, *seriously?*"

Tzarcyzk frowned in the background.

Guy replied enthusiastically.

"*YES!* I know, right? Can you believe it?"

"Oh, I believe it, all right."

Captain Paul threw all of the cards at Guy.

Guy got very scared all of a sudden.

Captain Paul grabbed him by the robe with one hand and pulled him closer so he was looking him right in the eyes.

"I believe that you've stolen Lieutenant Commander Tzarcyzk's notes and tried to pass them off as your own." Captain Paul's nostrils flared. "But what bothers me even *more,* is that you thought I was *stupid enough* to buy it."

Guy got really worried.

"If everyone else is like you from this 'Land of Ports', then to hell with it! I hope when Ragnarök comes it is wiped off the face of the Earth!"

Captain Paul raised his fist to punch Guy, and the cowering hipster closed his eyes and braced for it.

Then a voice rang out from out of nowhere, catching the whole crew off guard.

"EARTH?!" a man shouted, from near the ship's entrance.

He stepped out into the light.

"I think you mean... PLANET HITLER!"

Everyone gasped.

"HITLER!" Captain Paul shouted, letting go of Guy.

"HEY!" Guy cried, falling on his ass with a thud.

"How did *you* get out of your cell?" Paul asked.

"SIEG HIEL!" Hitler shouted, meaning *A man in a white lab coat let me out and then injected me with methamphetamine and told me that if I destroyed you all, I would rule the world.*

Tzarcyzk actually caught all of that.

Just like the prophecy! he thought.

"FUCK YOU, HITLER!" Paul shouted, and then addressed his crew. "Alright team, let's kill this bastard! Get your lazer pistols ready and fire at will."

Everyone started shooting lazers at Hitler, except for New Frankenstein who was just smacking his on the side, saying, "How do you work this thing?"

Hitler dodged all the lazer blasts with incredible speed, and ran towards the crew.

"CLEAR OFF, YOU WANKER!" Nigel shouted, shooting an awesome lazer beam with such precision that it went straight for Hitler.

But Hitler just leapt straight into the air, jumping clear over it, and came flying straight at the crew from a hundred feet away. Everyone shot their lazer rifles up at him as he soared through the air like a Nazi cannonball, too fast to hit.

"Everyone find cover!" Paul commanded, thinking that Hitler would land with such force it would shake the ground.

But it didn't. They were in the bay of a huge metal space station. It was pretty durable.

Hitler landed near New Frankenstein, who was still trying to get his lazer gun to work.

"*It must be jammed...*" he said, still looking down at it, not even noticing Hitler lunging straight at him.

"JEWISH BEAST!" Hitler yelled.

New Frankenstein was not only terrified, but also a little hurt. *Jewish beast,* he thought sadly, and frowned.

But then it seemed like the lazer pistol was suddenly working, as it started glowing red like it was charging.

"Ah-*ha!*" New Frankenstein exclaimed, and pointed the lazer at Hitler, with a smile on his face.

Hitler snatched the gun from his hands and took a bite out of it. Red electricity crackled around the gun like lightning, shot through Hitler's face and coursed beneath his skin. Hitler didn't flinch; he just kept staring at New Frankenstein and chewing on his lazer gun, taking big bites out of it and swallowing, red lazer plasma dribbling out the corners of his mouth.

New Frankenstein was aghast. Hitler's eye glowed red, as if lazer-charged.

"Frankenstein!" Paul shouted. "Get out of the way so we can get a clear shot!"

New Frankenstein ducked and hugged the floor.

But before anyone could get a shot, Hitler shot lazers out of his eyes at all the weapons with lightning speed, exploding them in their hands, burning them.

"*Ow ow ow!*" Nigel said, waving his hands around really fast to cool them off, looking girly.

Captain Paul took the hilt of his lazer sword off of his belt, which was lying nearby because he wasn't wearing it, he was just wearing a nice fluffy white bath robe instead, like the kind you get at the spa, and he gripped it with both hands and turned it on, and a really cool looking blue lazer beam shot out of it, and Paul held it up at the ready like a true warrior.

"Everyone stand back!" he shouted. "I'll take care of this German fool!"

Paul was a great swordsman, but Hitler on meth was still too fast for him. With every strike of his lazer sword, Hitler ducked or dodged it. He couldn't keep up! Hitler was on too much meth! Hitler eventually just pounced on the Viking and they both fell to the ground in a struggle as Paul tried to raise his lazer sword up to Hitler's neck to cut through it, but Hitler pushed the sword back away from him with all of his strength. Even without meth, Paul was still the stronger man, and the lazer was less than an inch away from the German's throat when Adolf Hitler shot a hot lazer blast out of his eyes and mouth straight at Paul's face. The Viking's screams were muffled by the endless barrage of lazer vomit that Hitler spewed upon him like lava as he held him down. Paul's lazer sword turned off as he stopped struggling, hands twitching.

And then he suddenly kicked the lazer beast off of him. Adolf Hitler tumbled away across the floor. He righted himself, crouching on all fours, and wiped the lazer drool from his mouth, smiling.

Paul held his hands up to his face, and tried to get up. He stumbled at first, and got back down on one knee. But he wouldn't give up, and stood up straight. Paul the Viking rubbed his face with his hands, hot lazer juice squeezing through his fingers. He rubbed and rubbed until the lazer juice started phasing out and disappearing. He scooped more off his face and shook it off his hands like it was nothing.

When he was finally done, he removed his hands from his face and revealed it to the crew, who were expecting him to be hideously deformed. But instead, Captain Paul had a perfectly trimmed red beard, which nicely form-fit to his face, accentuating his best features like his strong jawline. Also, his long hair was gone, and he was left with only the best and most attractive haircut imaginable, parted to one side in a perfect style. His bright blond hair shone like a ray of beautiful starshine.

"*Oh, Captain!*" Papillon squealed. "*You look so handsome!*"

"I agree!" Nigel said. "That is one good-looking man right there!"

Everyone gathered around him, wanting to

touch his hair and feel his face, showering him with nice compliments.

"Oh geez you guys," Paul blushed. "Thanks!"

"Did you forget about me?" Hitler asked, menacingly, from where they left him.

"Yes, we totally did, thank you," Paul said, not even looking in his enemy's direction.

"Well, you'll be sorry!" Hitler warned, and took up an attack stance as if to charge at the crew, and then added, "You'll be sorry if it's the last thing I do, or my name isn't *ADOLF HIT*—"

Hitler's battle cry was quickly cut off by the sound of a loud lazer blast. Hitler fell forward, flat on his face, with black smoke billowing out of his back. Behind him, Engineer Fred stood in the doorway to the ship, holding up his lazer rifle victoriously, having shot the meth-fueled German in the back.

"Derf!" Captain Paul smiled. "I thought you were dead!"

But wait a second, Tzarcyzk thought, *none of us thought he was dead. When we left the ship he was still alive.*

The crew ran over to greet him and congratulate him on killing Hitler.

"Great shot, mate!" Nigel said. "Couldn't have done it better myself."

"But how?" Paul asked. "You were just a skeleton when we left you."

Did the crew hit a timewarp that I missed or something? Tzarcyzk thought to himself.

"Yeah!" Papillon added. "How did you come back?"

"DERF IN TIMESTORM," the caveman replied, not talking eloquently anymore like he had before when he evolved.

Maybe he devolved too? Tzarcyzk wondered.

"Alright crew," Captain Paul said. "Let's get back on the ship and get out of here. This place sucks."

They all followed the captain back on the ship.

When Tzarcyzk passed by Derf, he asked, "How?"

The caveman replied, "*PLOTHOLE.*"

Oh, Tzarcyzk thought. *That makes perfect sense.*

CHAPTER TWENTY-SEVEN
ANCIENT ALIENS

The crazy LSD having long worn off, and Doctor Yes once again being forgotten, the crew sat on the bridge wondering what their next move should be.

"Tea time!" Nigel shouted. "That's it. That's exactly what we need!"

"Very good, Number One!" Captain Paul said, happy that someone finally thought of something.

"Gay Guy," the captain pointed at the hipster. "Two carafes of Earl Grey, piping hot."

"Aye aye, Captain," Guy said unenthusiastically, no more fight left in him.

"So..." Counselor Soo wondered. "Are we going to try to find our way home now?"

"Do we even want to go home?" Captain Paul asked. "I'm getting really used to this."

"Perhaps we could just figure out a way back and then check up on things," Commander Dickinson suggested. "And then we could decide if we want to go back or not."

"THERE IS NO WAY BACK!" shouted Doctor Yes, suddenly appearing on their viewscreen.

"BY ODIN'S BEARD!" Paul exclaimed, only slightly startled this time.

Tzarcyzk just looked back at him and shook his head.

Vikings... he thought.

"Did you forget about me?!" Doctor Yes asked.

"No sir," Tzarcyzk explained. "Well, I mean *yes*. Yes *and* no. See, whenever you reappear, you automatically create a paradox, leading us all to remember everything about you."

"Yeah," Guy said, returning with the tea. "And you're a dick. All experimenting on us all the time and shit." He poured the captain a cup and then looked up at the viewscreen and said, "Fuck you."

"Yeah," Papillon said. "We're, like, *tired*, man. We want to go home."

"Well," Doctor Yes said. "You're not going *anywhere!*"

"OH, SHUT UP!" Paul yelled, jumping out of his captain's chair to get closer to the viewscreen to confront him.

Guy accidentally got in the way and the tea tray slammed against his chest. The porcelain carafe shattered and scalding hot tea spilled down the front of his robe down to his penis.

"HEY!" Guy screamed. "*OW!* MY DICK!!"

"SHUT UP, GUY!" the captain yelled. "I'm going to tell this fucker a thing or two."

"Well," Doctor Yes said. "I'm waiting."

"OK, first thing—we're not just idle playthings for your wild amusement or something, and TWO," Paul said, holding up two fingers, pausing to think, "we want new uniforms!"

"Yeah!" Papillon shouted, excited about the prospect.

"Pip pip!" Nigel said. Whatever that means.

"THERE IS NO WAY BACK!" Doctor Yes shouted, again.

"Uh, yeah..." Paul said. "You already said that."

"DID YOU FORGET ABOUT ME?" the Doctor shouted once more, and then his eyes went in different directions and his head twitched.

"THERE IS N-NO-NO-NO-NO WA-WAY-WAY-WAY-WAY BACK," he repeated.

"Oh my god!" Tzarcyzk-616 cried. "He's stuck in a timeloop!"

"All hands to battle stations!" Captain Paul commanded. "Prepare for a timestorm!"

Everyone sat down and strapped themselves in.

New Frankenstein got confused and said, "Uh, guys? I don't really know what I'm supposed to be doing. By battle stations do you mean stand at this console and press buttons? I don't really know what any of them mean, you know."

Doctor Yes shook his head and blubbered.

"There *is* no timestorm," he said lucidly. "There is only *pain. And suffering!*"

"Right, right..." Commander Dickinson said, rolling his eyes. "Bugger off."

"Didn't you wonder why there were only a dozen or so crew members on the space station you were just on?" Doctor Yes asked.

"That one we just presumably have been flying away from in our ship ever since we left?" Captain Paul asked.

"Yes, that one."

"We just assumed they were mostly all inside of those ships we exploded during the lazer battle."

"No, that was a fully manned space station."

"OK, so where'd they go? Are we going to have to fight them again?"

"Christ, can we just go home?" Papillon asked.

"Not yet."

"BLOODY HELL, just show us already!" Nigel yelled, fed up.

"Very well! *Behold!*"

Doctor Yes changed the viewscreen to show what was occurring outside.

Planet XXX, which they were leaving behind, was apparently being pulled inside of an even larger space station. This one was shaped like a pyramid and had a large red eye at the top of its peak.

"Hey, it's a jumbo sized version of that thing we saw when we were trippin'!" Papillon said.

"And not only is it sucking Planet XXX in," Paul said, "but we're getting pulled back in as well!"

"Oh no!" New Frankenstein said worriedly. "I hope this isn't because I pressed the wrong button!"

New Frankenstein had pressed the wrong button, and it accidentally deleted this whole chapter. And then they all started back at where they began, back on board with the effects of the LSD wearing off.

CHAPTER TWENTY-SEVEN
ANCIENT ALIENS

Back on board the Star Smasher, the crew sat comfortably in the chairs on the bridge in their soft bath robes, sipping their nice hot cups of Earl Grey tea.

"That was fast," the captain noted. "Thank you, Guy."

Fuck you, Guy thought but didn't say out loud, still mad over the captain almost hitting him.

"My pleasure, Captain!" Guy said, fake smiling.

Suck up, Tzarcyzk thought.

"Alright crew, let's get out of here," Captain Paul commanded.

"Lieutenant Derf?" he asked the caveman, sitting at the helm.

"Derf make ship go."

Derf put the ship in drive and slowly piloted the Star Smasher out of the bay of the ISIS space station, which they have labeled *Planet XXX*.

It actually had a cooler name than that, but it was only written in squiggly lines on all of the stationary in the bay's offices, and Tzarcyzk's translator app on his handheld scanner was on the fritz, and plus he didn't care because Planet XXX had a nice ring to it anyway, so...

Once the ship was out of the bay and space bound, an alert rang out over the sound system.

"*Uh-oh,*" Nigel sighed, blowing on his hot cup of tea. "Not the *bad sound* again."

"Lieutenant Commander?" Captain Paul asked Tzarcyzk-616.

"A large unidentified object seems to be arriving in the direct vicinity."

"On screen!"

An enormous space pyramid, much larger than Planet XXX, was spinning towards them. Its great red eye stayed fixed at its peak, while the rest of it spun around and around beneath it. It seemed to create a strange vortex effect, beaming green rings of energy in a constant wave beneath its base.

"Do you think we can find any more acid?" Papillon asked. "This looks pretty cool."

"I think we still have those mushrooms left in the galley, babe," Nigel said.

"Captain?" he asked.

"Yes, Number One."

"Permission to order Guy to go to the galley and fetch us our alien mushrooms?"

"Permission granted."

"HEY!" Guy said.

"Guy, be a good lad and run off and fetch those mushrooms, will you?" Nigel said.

Guy grumbled.

"Sure thing, Mr. Dickinson," he said, looking down at his feet.

"THAT'S COMMANDER DICKINSON TO YOU, YOU LITTLE SHIT!" Nigel yelled at him, throwing his hot cup of tea in his face.

Guy screamed and ran off the bridge crying.

"Lieutenant Commander Tzarcyzk?" the captain asked. "Any readings?"

"Yes, Captain," Tzarcyzk's eyes darted back and forth superfast as he scanned the incoming information on his computer screen. "They seem to be charging a device."

"Goddamn it," Captain Paul said. "It's not that lazer eye, is it? That's like the biggest lazer ever. I hate that thing."

"It does look pretty cool though," Papillon noted.

"Agreed, but still..."

"No, Captain," Tzarcyzk replied. "They do not appear to be charging the lazer eye."

"Then what, Tzarcyzk?"

"It's their tractor beam."

A sudden burst of purple light enveloped them and the ship stalled and got stuck in the incredible force beam.

"Oh, goddamn it!" Paul cursed. "Not again!"

Paul shook his head, and looked at Tzarcyzk, who had his finger up as if he was about to add something.

"Don't say it!" Paul asked.

"We're being pulled in," Tzarcyzk said, putting his hand down and getting back to his computer readings.

"Fuck!" Captain Paul yelled.

Captain Paul looked at it all unfold on the

viewscreen, as they were caught helplessly in the pull.

"And why does it have to be purple?" Paul asked no one in particular. "I fucking hate purple."

Guy arrived back on the bridge with two big bowls of alien mushrooms.

The captain grabbed a handful and sat back down in his chair.

"Well, everyone. Just sit back and relax and eat some mushrooms."

He said it as more of a suggestion than a command.

God, I love the captain, Nigel thought. *He's so cool.*

Guy walked around with the mushrooms so everyone could grab a handful.

"Let's see where this goes," Captain Paul said, and they all watched the ancient alien pyramid get closer into view, as they ate alien mushrooms from another planet, aboard their alien starship that apparently once belonged to ISIS.

It couldn't be more interesting.

CHAPTER TWENTY-EIGHT
PYRAMID

Things were about to get much more interesting.

The crew were tripping balls by the time they were inside the pyramid, being led up a pathway by pyramid-headed muscle men holding electric tridents. The winding path inclined through a great glowing hall, shimmering gold, nothing beneath it but pitch black oblivion. Far ahead, at the path's destination, an array of lights leaked over the landing, changing colors, from green to red to blue to orange to yellow and back to green again.

A computer-like voice blared overhead, as if from heavenly loudspeakers. It spoke these words: "The civilizations of the past have been used as the foundation of the civilization of today. Because of this, the world keeps looking toward the past for guidance. Too many people are following the past. In this new space age, this is dangerous. The past is dead and those who are following the past are doomed to die and be like the past. It is no accident that those who die are said to have passed since those who have passed are past."

"What the fuck does that mean?!" New Frankenstein asked, frightened. "It doesn't make any sense! What's with all that light up

there? *What's happening!?* OW!"

A pyramid-headed guard zapped New Frankenstein with the end of his lazer trident.

"Calm down, Frankenstein," Papillon said. "You're killing the mood."

"Yeah," Nigel said. "And that was a great message, mate. *Totally* deep."

When they arrived at the top of the platform, a tiny brown alien man in a pointed hat sat upon a golden throne. He looked quite odd. Pretty much like Sil from the twenty-second season of Doctor Who, when Colin Baker played the Doctor. Just google him to see what he looks like. My editor won't let me include a photo here, even though I wanted to really bad.

"What the fuck?!" Guy asked. "Is this like the Wizard of Oz and shit?"

"I don't think that they are wizards," Captain Paul said, instead of "shut up, Guy!" for once.

"We are *not* wizards, young Paul," the wizard-like alien said.

"We are the future. You are the past. All of you," he motioned down to the group, who stood lined up before him at the foot of the stairs to his throne, with armed guards at their sides.

"You're all from the past," the alien said. "From different times."

I'm not from the past though, Tzarcyzk thought. *Hell, I'm probably from further in the future than he is.*

He wanted to speak up and say that but decided it

would probably not be in his best interest. Besides, he wanted to hear what the alien had to say.

"You have all been gathered together for a reason. Do you know what reason?" the alien asked.

"We do not," Captain Paul answered. "We were all plucked from our timelines and put on that ship together by..." he continued, trying to remember his name, "...let's call him *'the man in the white lab coat'*, for an experiment the reasons of which he has never fully revealed."

"Is this the man in the white lab coat you are talking about?" the alien asked, pointing up to a gilded cage hanging from the ceiling by a chain, suddenly illuminated by a spotlight. A terrified Doctor Yes stood in the cage, holding onto the bars.

"*Help me...*" he pleaded.

"Doctor Yes!" the team shouted, surprised to see him up there.

"Doctor who?" the man in the white lab coat asked.

"Doctor Yes," Nigel said. "That's your name, isn't it?"

"My name is Dr. Kyle Robertson."

"HA!" the alien leader said. "He made you call him Doctor Yes?"

"Yes, he did," Paul confirmed.

"Sometimes he made us call him 'Y'," Papillon added, wondering whether she was just hallucinating the alien as tiny or whether he was actually really tiny.

He looks like a baby, she thought.

"Dr. Kyle Robertson is *mine*," the alien boasted.

"It was *I* who sent him. It was *I* who pulled the strings." The alien made puppeteering hand gestures, like he was pulling the strings. "He was my *puppet*."

"Yeah," Paul said. "We get the picture."

"So, you were the one who gathered us all?" Nigel asked. "Why?"

"The reason would be beyond your human comprehension."

"But how about Tzarcyzk-616?" Paul asked. "He's not human. I'm sure it's not beyond *his* comprehension. Right, Lieutenant Commander?"

"Correct, Captain," Tzarcyzk confirmed.

"Then let's hear it," Paul said.

Tzarcyzk stepped forward, and pulled out his note cards. There he had it all completely laid out from beginning to end, several thousand words that completely detailed the connection between the aliens, LSD experiments, time travel, terrorist agents, and even *Star Trek*.

Tzarcyzk cleared his throat, and was about to read, when someone screamed, "TIMESTORM!"

"Another timestorm?!" Papillon said. "I *must* be tripping!"

"But he was just getting to the good stuff!" Nigel said. "I *have to* know!"

But time vortexes swarmed and swarmed and whirled around each member of the crew, and took them away.

"STOP THEM!" the ancient alien commanded. "THIS IS A TOTAL COPOUT!"

But it was too late; the timestorm had whisked away the crew and disappeared with them.

"DR. KYLE!" the alien shouted.

The Doctor looked over at him.

"DO SOMETHING!"

The Doctor, with a blank expression, said, "We don't belong here. It's time we went back to our own times."

And the timestorm wrapped around the Doctor too, and he disappeared.

"But I haven't even revealed my master plan yet!" The alien held his hands up to his face and screamed, "*NOOOO!*"

The pyramid-headed men turned around, and in single file, marched back down the winding metallic pathway. As they descended, the light coming from the platform slowly dimmed.

CHAPTER TWENTY-NINE
HOME

Paul woke up in his bed at home. The mattress, stuffed with crunchy but soft hay, brought familiarity. Outside he could hear the chickens clucking. He got up and stretched, then thought, *some dream*. He opened the door and walked outside to take a leak near some bales of hay outside the farmhouse.

Ah, Norway, he thought. *Where a true Viking, like me, belongs.*

He went to wash his face in a bowl of rinse water nearby and suddenly noticed his reflection. His hair was short and his beard trimmed to near perfection.

Just like in my dream! he thought, surprised.

Then he heard a man screaming from far away, like a girl, and the sound was increasing like it was getting closer and closer. But from where? Paul looked around and there was no one else in sight. It was just him and the chickens.

Then the bale of hay next to him nearly exploded as something hit it from above like a ton of bricks.

A skinny little man rolled out of it, and yelled, "JESUS CHRIST!"

The man got up and brushed himself off. He apparently had fallen from the sky.

"Where the fuck am I?" he started bitching and complaining. "What the hell is this shithole? Who the fuck are you? The cover model for Medieval GQ magazine?"

"SHUT UP, GUY!" Paul shouted.

"PAUL?!" Guy screamed. "Is that you?!"

"Ha! Yes!" Paul smiled jovially. "Yes it is! I guess it was not a dream after all."

"Where are we?"

Paul looked around.

"We are at my home, in Norway. It looks like the same morning when I left."

"It looks like shit."

"Fuck you, Guy!"

"Sorry, sorry. It just doesn't look like there's anything to do nearby. I wish we had landed back in my era. At least we have internet."

Paul started remembering all the wondrous things he had discovered in the future. It was everything that he had wanted to discover. And now that he was home... home just didn't seem that special anymore.

"We have to get back," Paul said.

"Back to the ship?"

"Yes, I think it's where we belong."

"You mean *I* belong there too?" Guy asked, childlike.

"Of course, Guy. The ship wouldn't be the same without you."

Guy smiled. He guessed it was pretty cool to be in space. Why should he want to go back to Portland ever again? He was too hip for it now. He was pretty sure no one from Portland, Oregon had ever been to space and back again. That whole town was pretty gay, he thought. He was too cool to live there anymore. He was a spaceman.

"And what about me?" said a voice from around the corner, that sounded remarkably British.

"NIGEL!" Paul shouted.

"Hiya!" the Brit answered with a smile.

Paul ran up and gave him a great big bear hug. "You're here!"

"Well, I always did want to drop in and visit Norway."

"It *is* where our people come from, after all," Paul smiled at him, and put a big Viking helmet on his head.

Nigel blushed.

"You Earth people, always smiling," Tzarcyzk-616 said.

"TZARCYZK!" Paul yelled.

"Why are you always smiling? What do you have to be so happy about all the time?" he asked, and then smiled too. "You're just too amazing."

Paul ran over and gave Tzarcyzk a bear hug too.

"Good to see you again, Captain."

Nigel joined them and took off his Viking helmet.

"I think the Lieutenant Commander deserves this even more than I do, Captain."

But before he put it atop the young alien's head, he

[185]

noticed a name written on the inside of the helmet.

"Dickinson?" he said, reading it out loud.

"Yep!" Paul said. "That's the family name."

"But that's a *British* name."

"It is since my people last visited your country."

Paul smiled, "I'm sure there are lots of little Dickinsons running around the countryside these days."

Paul almost about keeled over with laughter.

"I've raped the shit out of your country," Paul said, laughing out loud. "Oh my god, I've raped it so hard."

Nigel was aghast.

"So, are we related?" he asked.

"Of course, we've got to be."

"Tzarcyzk?" Nigel asked. "Is this true?"

"A compulsory scan shows that you share almost all of the same DNA and Paul is your great-great-great-great-great-great-great-great-great-great-great-great-grandfather."

"But he buggered me when we were on mushrooms!"

"HA!" Guy shouted. "Where did you think the name 'Dickinson' came from?"

"Royalty?" Nigel wondered.

Guy laughed.

"No, dick-in-son. Dick-in-son? Putting your dick in your son? Get it?"

Nigel was shocked.

"That's not what it means!"

Paul laughed, and reassured him, "It's OK, Nigel.

A little incest never hurt anyone, as long as it's gay."

"Incest hurts plenty of people! It's terrible!" Nigel protested.

"Alright," Guy interrupted. "Let's move on already, we should talk about how we're going to find the rest of the crew and locate the Star Smasher."

"The rest of the crew will probably just fall out of the sky any time now," Paul said, dismissively.

And with that, New Frankenstein fell to solid ground. Followed by Derf, who landed right on top of him.

"Frankenstein! Derf!" Paul shouted.

"My name's not Frankenstein, you know," the tall, Frankenstein-headed man said. "I guess I never got a chance to introduce myself. My name is Robert Dickinson."

"Oh my god, Zarsh!" Guy said. "Are they related too?"

Tzarcyzk-616 scanned New Frankenstein.

"No. This time it's just a coincidence."

Guy frowned. That would have been cool.

"And what about you, Derf?" Paul asked. "Are you still Derf or Fred or what?"

"Derf."

"Do you want to go back in space with us too?"

"Derf miss Derk."

"Who's Derk?" Paul asked.

And then a big beast the size of a car suddenly fell out of the sky and rolled over on its back in front of the group and panted.

"DERK!" Derf shouted, and ran up to rub his pet Glyptodon's belly.

"Oh, I suppose that thing is his pet," Nigel noted. "But how'd *that* get here?"

"I just whipped up a timestorm!" Papillon said, coming from out of nowhere as well to greet the crew.

"COUNSELOR SOO!" the group greeted her excitedly, glad to see her.

"I was wondering when you were going to show up, babe," Nigel said, kissing her on the cheek.

"You can always count on me, darling," she said.

"Hey, how did you know how to whip up a timestorm?" Paul asked.

Papillon smiled. "I've been taking time courses. I've been training to be a *time master!* It's all in the future."

"You've been away longer than us?" Nigel asked.

"A bit longer, yes," a man said, suddenly walking down towards them out of thin air, like an angel.

"DOCTOR YES?" Paul shouted.

"Doctor Yes, *hmmmm…*" the man in the white laboratory coat pondered. "Sure, I'll go with it. It's kind of got a nice ring to it."

"Where's our ship? The Star Smasher?" Paul asked.

"Why, it's right here," Y said, and snapped his fingers.

The Star Smasher magically appeared behind him.

"I just had it cloaked, so it was invisible. We don't want the people of ancient Norway freaking out now, do we?"

A lot of people living nearby in ancient Norway immediately started freaking out at the sight of the massive spaceship.

"Ah, who cares," the Doctor said. "I got you guys new uniforms! Check 'em out!"

Everyone rushed up and grabbed their new uniforms and checked them out.

"Wow!" Paul said. "These are awesome!"

Doctor Yes clapped his hands together.

"All right then. Would everyone like to join me back on the S.S. Mashrue, where we can indulge in psychedelics, free love, and space exploration?"

"And don't forget the lazers!" Paul said, smiling. "The lazers are the best part."

"And there's one more thing," Tzarcyzk-616 said.

"What's that, Lieutenant Commander?" Captain Paul asked.

"The ancient aliens are still going to come to Earth and destroy Portland, and maybe the rest of the world, in the year 2026."

"Eh, fuck Portland," Guy said. "I'm so done with that place."

"But if they destroy Portland, they might destroy the rest of the world," Tzarcyzk argued.

"Well, then fuck the rest of the world."

"SHUT UP, GUY!" Captain Paul commanded.

"We have to stop them somehow," Tzarcyzk said. "But I need some time to come up with a plan."

"*We* need some time," Commander Dickinson said, putting his hand on the boy's shoulder. "We're a team."

Nigel smiled, and Tzarcyzk smiled back at him.

"Alright then, team!" Captain Paul smiled. "Let's get on board and set a course for Portland, Oregon, in the year of two-thousand and twenty-six!"

"But Tzarcyzk?" Paul asked.

"Yes, Captain?"

"Let's take the long way around," Paul smiled.

"Aye aye, Captain!"

And with that, the crew got back on board the Star Smasher, eager to explore space, discover new worlds, fight ominous alien threats for the sake of humanity, and most of all, love each other. The crew of the Star Smasher were more than a team — they were a *family*.

Except for Guy. Guy was gay.

"HEY!"

THE END

- Vince Kramer, Rockaway Beach, Oregon, Timedate: 2:25AM, April 16th, 2016

Vince Kramer's Top Ten Biography Ideas –

1. Secret message that you have to order a decoder ring to read.

2. The complete truth, nothing but.

3. Braggy, literary nerd bio.

4. Describe his Action Figures Fucking photography, which you can find on his tumblr @ vincekramer222.tumblr.com

5. Talk about where he's from (Philadelphia, Pennsylvania), his hair color (blond), eye color (green), and penis size (8").

6. Rip on Star Trek in 5,000 words or less, including details about how much he actually loves Star Trek, but Star Wars is still better.

7. Loving mention of his pet, a five foot long green iguana named Desmond Harrington, whom he lives with in Happy Valley, Oregon, along with his best friend Gary (human).

8. Make a shit list of all the people who have pissed him off over the years, and say they should be decapitated by ISIS.

9. Throw the word "gay" author in there somewhere. As if it's a struggle to be gay or something.

10. Mention his first two books – Gigantic Death Worm and Death Machines of Death, available from Eraserhead Press.